Sister Amnesia

For Gemma —
I hope you smile when
you read it.
Joan Albaully

Advance Praise for *Sister Amnesia*:

"Is it a mystery? Is it a science fiction novel? Or is it simply a study in faith? By the time you've finished *Sister Amnesia*, you may decide, as I did, that it's all of the above and more…an entertaining and humorous story with characters who stay with you even after you've come to the awe-inspiring end."…Dorothy Taylor, co-author of *Teaching English Language Learners: Strategies That Work*.

"Nuns, punk rockers, amnesia, aliens and baby goats! What more could you want? Sister Amnesia has it all—and it's packed into one seriously fun, rollicking romp of a read"…Mary Akers, award-winning author of *Women Up On Blocks*.

"Sister Jane's life is saved by a young punk woman, who hits her head and loses her memory. Who is she? Why is the ILA interested in her? Passive-aggressive Sister Magdalene, Brother Samuel, and French Sister Mimi try to help but soon discover an even bigger secret. The answers to both mysteries can only be found on high. A shockingly funny book about finding your true home-on earth or above"…Meg Davis, UK Agent.

"This is one Amnesia you'll never forget. Don't look for a better novel; you'll find Nun"…Jerry Reiter, author of *Live from the Gates of Hell*.

Sister Amnesia

Joan Albarella

Published by The Writer's Den

Buffalo, New York

The Writer's Den
Buffalo, New York

Published by The Writer's Den

www.angelfire.com/journal/garyearlross

Printed in the United States of America

ISBN: 978-0-578-03677-9

Cover Design and Art by Daniela Bagnoli

DEDICATION

This book is lovingly dedicated to Karen Whitney who reassured me that I was a writer and never refused to read one more draft. She was kindly diplomatic when she corrected my blatant spelling and grammatical errors and always laughed at my jokes.

ACKNOWLEDGMENTS

I wish to thank Meg Davis for her patience, understanding, and writing/publishing acumen. She never gave up but always gently directed me on to a better progression and product. I am forever indebted to her for the reassurance that quirky is really okay.

I also thank Gary Earl Ross and Mary Akers, both writers' writers willing to share their insights and the expertise they learned along the way.

I am indebted to Daniela Bagnoli for her contagious enthusiasm and creative talent. She brought the missing brightness to the whole project.

I also wish to acknowledge the support of the Mystery Writers of America who helped make this publication possible.

CHAPTER 1

It is summer in Syracuse and benevolent weather is unusual, but Jane sees the afternoon sky as a mother-of-pearl alpaca rug with blue and teal stripes. She studies it intently, focusing her mind on this curious meteorological phenomenon. The atypical temperate air brushes her face as it moves on a tranquil breeze.

Quite spontaneously, she throws her fist up into the air. "I can do this!" she confidently declares, but quickly slides her arm back down. "Perhaps with some help," she quietly adds.

She shakes her head and shoulders like a runner preparing for a race. This frees the doubt that binds her, and she takes a few steps closer to the "Recovery Community Clinic."

Facing the small brick building across the street, she finds her hands are sweating; her throat is dry; and she can't swallow. She scans the sky again, looking for a distraction from her symptoms. A speeding circular glint catches her attention. It moves quickly from horizon to horizon. *Maybe this is a sign?*

She looks for it again. *Or maybe it's just one of those spaceships that Culberth always mentioned. Maybe it's just another odd heavenly visitor.* She keeps stalling.

This is more difficult than I thought…but I can do it! Her fist flies into the air again. *I can walk right in there and make an appointment.*

Her hand slides to her side again, and she searches the sky for the silver glint. *This weather,* she stalls some more, *is no doubt due to the inscrutable synergy of God and Nature?* Her profundity causes an unexpected click in her brain. *Maybe it's due to something unnatural, something beyond God or nature. Maybe something bad is about to happen.*

This thought is enough to stop any progress. "We really don't need to worry about evil, even if it comes disguised." Sister Jane Dalton recites part of last Sunday's sermon. "We all have our angels and trusted ethereal beings. Although I haven't seen any, especially when I really needed them." She nonchalantly makes her aside. "It seems I have to help myself."

She holds the small cross around her neck and looks at the clinic still across the street. "I'm sorry, Lord, for being such a baby. I'm just scared. I know, I know. A woman in my position should not be scared." She squeezes her deep green eyes shut and prays. "Give me a little push, okay? I promise I'll stop complaining."

She looks to the heavens one last time, wondering about all the celestial detritus floating around in space. Then she steps off the curb and takes a giant misstep. She twists her ankle which pulls her attention painfully back to earth.

Weak ankles! The words shoot through her thoughts. *But that's from my other life, my past life.* She instinctively grabs her ankle.

These pain-driven thoughts run off, and she can't catch them. *Weak ankles! Weak ankles!* They explode like a Roman candle. Is this her message for the day? Can this be her epiphany? *Weak ankles! Weak ankles! Weak ankles!*

Jane pushes her salt and pepper, in-need-of-a-trim hair out of her eyes. *What's happening?* Her thoughts are now ping pong balls in play. *I can't move…I'm transfixed… transfixed in the middle of Genesee Street!*

She tilts her head to divert the sun bouncing off her wire-rimmed glasses. Oversized oblongs of cars, trucks, and buses blur past her. *Look both ways and always cross at the corner.* Jane doesn't need this untimely internal safety lesson.

"I always look both ways, and I never cross at the corner." She starts rubbing the offending limb. "Why walk that far? I know this is a busy street, but I've crossed in the middle a hundred times. I'm always careful, and I saw that truck. It was at least a block away and going way too fast, as usual."

The red Onondaga Beer truck was certainly far enough away when she started to cross the street but when that sudden, slicing pain shot through her ankle, well, that's when she instinctively stopped to seize the attacking appendage.

Full recognition reaches Sister Jane Dalton. She is stuck, in the pain, in the moment, in the middle of Genesee Street with a crazed beer truck speeding right at her"

Weak ankles! The thought jumps in again. These are not the words she expected to hear when her life or death moment arrived. She expected something uplifting, something spiritual, but all she gets is *Weak ankles!* These are the cautionary words of muscular Miss Tartar, her grammar school Physical Education teacher. This is what a PE teacher *would* say when you trip over your field hockey stick.

Jane's mind cavalierly wastes precious seconds commiserating over this poverty-stricken part of the city. A small group of multi-racial, multi-ethnic, rainbow people are waiting for a bus…and one of the colors of the rainbow screams at her.

"Jesus Christ, Lady! Get outta the street! Can't you see that friggin' truck comin?"

Who's screaming? Jane comes to attention. *Yes, those are the words I hoped I'd hear. Well, not all of those words.*

Her body is stuck in this dangerous place. It's too late. Even with her blurred vision, she sees the truck is only yards away. She starts to pray.

"Jesus Christ, lady! Holy crap!" The screaming rainbow is closer now. Both bodies grunt on contact, and two strong arms lift Jane off the highway and propel her back against the curb. Jane's side hits the concrete edge with full force and redirects her pain from her ankle to her ribs.

She can't breathe...can't catch her breath. She gasps for air while the oversized tires of the yellow-eyed, red monster screech past her and finally stop.

Her lungs are reassured that they still work, and she prays in short, quick breaths. "Thank you...Lord...Alleluia... Alleluia...I'm saved! Rescued by someone who calls on God and thinks even crap is holy. Perhaps he or she is an animist."

Jane is not thinking rationally. *My...my...my body is shaking...shaking for no reason.* She doesn't like to lose control. She is the elected Moderator of the Sisters of St. Francis Dupre. St. Francis would expect her to be calm and grateful for her deliverance, but her teeth keep chattering, and she wonders who saved her.

A pile of black leather lies two feet away. It's a black leather lump with no visible movement. What was an uplifting breeze pushing her to safety is now a still black bundle, except for an explosion of hot pink, green, and a sticky red around this unusual angel's head.

"I have to help." Jane groans in a painful attempt to stand, "Ohh!" She grabs her side. The brush-burns on her arms and the bloody scratches on her knees are peppered with dirt and gravel. All of her wounds are singing similar painful pronouncements.

Jane laboriously crawls to the leather mass. Rainbow people form a protective circle around the injured while a hooded youth uses his cell phone to call for help.

A gargantuan accumulation of male humanity jumps from the

cab of the beer truck and marches over. He bends down, face to face with Jane, and booms, "I had the light ya know. I never saw ya. What the hell were ya doin in the street? I can't stop dat fast. Are ya both okay?"

"We need some help." Jane's control is back and audible in her take-charge voice. She reaches over and realizes her guardian angel is a young woman. The hot pink and green are spikes of hair, very short hair. The sticky red is a pool of blood gathering on the edge of the concrete curb where the young woman's head is resting. Jane's heroine is face down and motionless.

Jane banishes any negative thoughts. She feels protective and wants to lift the pink, green, and red head off the curb. A shrill ambulance siren stops her. "Thank God," Jane says to the emergency vehicle maneuvering alongside of her.

The young woman is first to be rolled onto a gurney. She has a large cut on her forehead and sticky red stripes trickle down her face.

She's a young, white woman. That's how they'll report it on the six o'clock news. Jane knows that every member of her Order watches the six o'clock news. Accidents are big news in Syracuse, especially if a nun is involved. They'll say, "An elderly nun and a young white woman were almost hit by a truck." Jane doesn't like the sound of that even if she did just tell the EMT when she was born. "Yes, I'm sixty- years-old. Yes, I'm a nun. Ouch! Yes, my ribs hurt very much."

Jane looks over at the young woman. It's hard to tell her age with all the blood. But Jane does notice her earrings. A small pistol and a large cross in her left ear and a star-shaped diamond in her nose. "I've never seen anything like that," Jane mumbles to the EMT who thinks she's praying.

The odd hair coloring is not a problem for Jane. She sees lots of orange hair. Several of her Sisters work in secular business offices and, like their coworkers, try to hide their grey. They save money dying their own hair, but often something goes wrong. Jane remembers struggling not to laugh when both Sister Louise and Sister Carla, who work for the Child Protection Agency, appeared at morning mass looking like carrot heads.

This woman's hair is different though. It must be the cut. She has a buzz cut or brush-cut. Jane remembers this boy's style from when she was young. That's what Elvis got when he went into the Army. Elvis was on the cover of *Life* magazine getting his head shaved.

"It seems a little strange," Jane mumbles again. "This poor woman has an Elvis Army haircut and a chain attaching her nose to her ear."

"Please lie back on the gurney, Ma'am—I mean Sister." The EMT gently pushes Jane to a prone position. She tries to overhear the other EMT who is working on the young woman.

"She's breathing okay. Pressure's good… Pulse's good."

Relief moves down Jane's body, and she sinks into the gurney. She thanks God again and lets her heart continue to pray for the young woman's recovery.

******

International Intelligence Agent Edward Whittington wraps his trench coat around his new blue suit and cautiously sits on the dusty office chair. He takes out his cell phone and swings his legs up on the desk all in one move. He scrolls down and pushes the number, never taking his eyes off a nickel-sized spider wrapping a web around a still-struggling moth.

"It's Whittington. We picked up something big on visual. Yeah, just outside of Paris again." He expertly aims and then flicks a loose paperclip at the large spider. "No one saw anything or that's what they're saying. We're not sure. We have the ship. Oh yeah, that sector is a hotbed of activity. We've had a group of our best stationed there for years. What?"

He drops his feet to the ground and shoots up to a standing position. "I don't care how many gold stars are on your shoulder! You have no jurisdiction in our work. This is a courtesy call. I'm not obligated to be courteous. Yeah, that's right."

He sits back down. "We found three dead ones. They're already in Nevada, but we think one or more got away." He flicks another paperclip at the spider, this time breaking a large section of the web. "It's very important. That's why I'm calling." He shakes his head in frustration. "I want you to send someone to Camp Eleven. Yeah, to the camp! I want them to get some answers from an old woman named Culberth. No, I don't know her number. Look it up! She's French and knows that area. She's seen them and may know something about this one."

He listens to a response he obviously doesn't like. "I have a better idea. Send Anastasia. I don't care how many times she's been reprimanded. Send her; she'll get the old Frenchwoman to talk. We need that information." He slams down the phone.

*****

Sister Jane is wheeled into the Emergency Room and spends an hour answering questions while staring at the off-white ceiling. She is taken to radiology for x-rays and finally transferred to an examination table in a small curtained cubicle.

A teenage-looking man calling himself Dr. John comes in and listens to her heart and lungs. He pushes and squeezes various groups of her muscles and bones and holds up two oversized x-rays.

"You have two badly bruised ribs. . . Mrs. . . . . Mrs. . . ." Dr. John checks his chart. "Oh, I'm so sorry, Sister Jane." He becomes overly solicitous. "We don't tape bruised ribs, Sister. You'll have some discomfort, so just rest for a few weeks until they heal."

Jane protests. "I can't just rest. I have work to do."

"What kind of work do you do?" Dr. John asks naively.

"I don't just sit around praying all day." Jane is annoyed. "I'm in charge of our local Order. I do a lot of paper work, speeches, travel, meetings, meetings, and more meetings."

"I see." The doctor finally does see but continues his caveat. "You can't do any of that for at least a few weeks, and you better take it easy for a few after that. You're going to be in some pain, Sister. It's not just your ribs, but your arms and legs are lacerated. They need to stay clean to avoid infection."

He holds the x-rays up to the overhead light again. "You also have a sprained ankle which you'll have to soak for a day or two. And you need to stay off that foot."

He makes several notes in her chart, smiles and glibly adds, "You must have weak ankles."

This classic reminder, this cold blast from the past, is not appreciated, but Jane knows better than to say something that might be perceived as out of character. She quietly asks, "Could someone please call Sister Mary Magdalene to pick me up?"

Dr. John cheerily responds. "One of the nurses will call her right away." He finishes writing in her chart and becomes extremely serious. "The police want to speak to you Sister, about the woman who was with you."

"Is she all right? Has something happened to her?" Jane's imagination kicks into gear.

The doctor tries to be reassuring. "She's all right, medically. I mean she took a really hard blow to her head, needed eight stitches...but there is a problem."

Good Lord! Jane's fear builds again. *She's brain damaged! She's crippled! She's irreparably harmed all because she saved my life!*

Dr. John sees Jane's concern. "It's not that bad, really. She has amnesia, that's all. It's very common when you have a hard blow to the head. It can be a temporary condition." He smiles. "Researchers think it may be related to the swelling, but no one knows for sure."

Jane likes the optimism of this teenage doctor, and she gives him a smile back.

Dr. John continues in the same soft voice. "The problem is she has no identification, no purse or wallet, or papers of any kind. The police want to know who she is."

As he finishes this last statement, Jane notices the legs of a uniformed police officer beneath the curtains of her cubicle. "Can I come in now, Doc?" A deep, muffled voice asks.

The doctor quickly wraps a sheet around Jane, bundling her up like a shy papoose. Obviously still unconvinced that her appearance reflects propriety, he takes her charcoal-grey jacket and drapes it around the sheet. None of her hospital gown is now visible. The doctor still wears his friendly smile and quietly asks, "Is it all right to let the police officer in now?"

Jane nods and the doctor opens the curtain. As the officer enters, Dr. John waves goodbye. The officer is short and round, a walrus-looking man uncharacteristically holding Jane's purse under his arm.

"Sister Jane Anne Dalton?" He speaks with what appears to be extra amounts of saliva swishing in his mouth, and he sounds like he left his upper plate at home.

"Yes, I'm Sister Jane Dalton," the papoose responds.

"We found yer purse, Sister." He hands it to her while she struggles to free a hand and grasp it. "But we got a little problem." He sloshes again.

"Is there something I can help you with?" Jane can't help staring at his mouth.

"We don't have any identification for dat other woman. Nothin' on her person and nothin' at the accident scene." He smacks his lips. "Do you know who she is?"

"No, no I don't." Jane pauses before giving a more precise

explanation. "I never saw her until after she pushed me out of the way, until she was unconscious." Jane starts to shake again. A dark blanket of guilt engulfs her. Guilt is an old, familiar friend.

She takes a breath in and lets it out slowly, struggling to shake off this uncomfortable feeling. "I don't mean to sound flippant officer, but did you try to ask her what her name is?" Jane knows from experience that the obvious often isn't.

"Yeah," he sloshes a little longer for emphasis. "We asked." He looks directly at Jane. "Ya know she's got amnesia, don't ya, Sister?"

"Yes, I was told about the amnesia. I guess I thought she might remember something."

"Oh, she does. They always do." The officer exudes experience now. He hikes up his pants. "She remembers how to go to the bathroom and that's good. Some of 'em forget, ya know. They just wet all over."

Jane feels this information was not worth sharing. "I didn't know that. No, I didn't." She tries her question again. "Did she remember her name, along with the bathroom, I mean?"

He takes another healthy suck. "She told us her name is Hershey. Yep, Hershey Ghirardelli." He gives a hearty laugh and reveals that he did indeed forget his upper plate. He has absolutely no top teeth.

Jane thinks this is an unusual name, perhaps Italian. She's about to comment, but the officer interrupts. "We know that's not her name. They all try to come up with somethin'. They get upset not rememberin' and try to make some connections."

"Are you sure that's not her name?" Jane suddenly gets goose bumps on her arms, another old response to danger.

"Dat's not her name." He's more self-assured now. "She's got two candy bar wrappers in her pocket, a Hershey bar and a Ghirardelli bar. Dat's the name of da candy."

He turns to leave. "Thanks for yer help, Sister. We`ll need to bother you once more. We got the truck driver's statement, now we need yours. You can give it to me here or come down to the station when yer feeling better."

"What will happen to that young woman?"

Officer Walrus hikes up his pants again. "Oh, they'll keep her here tonight, if there's enough room. Maybe they'll push her out later this afternoon."

Jane's mouth drops open, and the officer anticipates what she is about to ask. "They won't really push her out," he guffaws. "We'll have to put her over in the Holding Center or get her admitted to the county mental hospital. Can't let her wander around in that condition with no ID. She could be considered a vagrant. We'll run her fingerprints through our database, but you gotta be sensitive to vagrant's rights."

"Isn't the Holding Center the jail?" Jane's voice goes up a pitch. "A jail or the county hospital, that's where she'll go?" A current of fear moves from Jane's brain to her stomach and settles in a familiar knot. "She isn't a criminal, and she isn't crazy."

"Don't get yourself worked up Sister." He slurps rapidly. "We get cases like this a lot. Once they put her description in the paper and on TV, somebody'll come and get her. In the meantime, we lock'em up for their own good."

Jane is distrustful of this man. The ache in her stomach starts to throb. "For her own good?" Dark memories of locked rooms and fearful nights flit in and out of her mind. "Did you say locking her up is for her own good?"

"Yeah." He feels defensive now. "You may not realize it, but there's all kinds of bad people out there . . . people who can take advantage of this woman."

"So that's why you'll lock her up?" Jane's voice has a bite to it now. "And no one will take advantage of her in jail or in the mental hospital? Is that what you're saying?"

He thinks for a minute. "Well, I suppose anythin' can happen, but we don't have much choice."

He's not sure why they are arguing, but he doesn't like to lose. "She has some money. In fact, she had a roll of two hundred dollars in her pocket. Now, I don't want to think about how she got that. So ya see Sister, jail is probably best, until some..." He takes a marked pause. "Some friend or family comes to claim her."

Small electric jolts run up and down Jane's arms. Her edginess is growing. Is it the officer's demeaning attitude or her personal knowledge of being locked up? "With that much money, she's certainly not a vagrant."

Jane squiggles to the edge of the table to advance the discussion. "What if I claim her and take her home with me...back to our convent, at least until someone comes for her?"

The officer quickly responds. "That's not a good idea. You don't know anythin' about this woman. She may not be the type you want to take to a convent."

His concern sounds sincere and professional, but Jane no longer wants to be logical. She allows an almost other-worldly force to take over. "I'm going to take her home with me."

The officer nods reluctantly. "I can see you've made up yer mind. I've dealt with enough stubborn women to know that. I can't stop ya, but I'll repeat my warning. I think yer asking for trouble. There's something about that amnesia woman that feels like trouble."

He points upward. "America's enemies don't always come from across the oceans, and they don't all look like gas station owners. If ya know what I mean."

Jane is speechless. This man is a reincarnation of her prejudiced Uncle Harold, who always thought the communists were taking over the country.

With his indignation now under control, the officer continues.

"I'll get her story to the news sources. Maybe you'll get lucky and someone will show up tonight…or maybe no one will show up ever. Have you thought about that?"

Jane makes eye contact with him. "If that proves to be the case, would she be spending the rest of her life in jail or the county hospital?"

The officer doesn't flinch. "Only 'til she remembers who she is, if she ever does." He wipes his mouth with the back of his hand. "She's yer problem now."

He starts to leave but turns back. "I'll tell the doctor yer takin' custody of her. Leave yer number in case someone comes looking for her. But . . . don't sit by yer phone waiting."

CHAPTER 2

Jane cautiously slides off the examining table and arduously fastens each button of her wrinkled white blouse. She must rest several times but needs to get dressed, so she can leave. She wonders if her accident is a portent of what is yet to come, especially regarding the mysterious young woman. She leans exhausted against the table, and her attention is drawn to three sets of legs under the cubicle. The torsos are not visible, but Jane knows who they are.

"Come in! Just come in! I'm in here!" Jane speaks louder than necessary. Through the opening, in a line of marked precision, come her three convent companions, looking very much like ducks in a row.

Yes, Sister Mary Magdalene is always first, Jane mentally observes. *Our mercurial Magdalene can be loyal and loving. Unfortunately, she's often more crabby and critical. A retired teacher, Second-in-Convent Command, and always impeccably dressed with her pressed navy-blue blazer in perfect line with her matching A-line skirt. She's frowning as usual, and I think that wrinkled brow makes her look all of sixty-two years of age.*

Ah, Brother Samuel, Jane continues her silent observations. *He looks so nice… neatly pressed navy-blue suit. Not an official Brother yet, but one of our few St. Francis of Dupre Associates, an excellent lay member of our Order.….adjusted well to convent life and doing well in his abbreviated novitiate.*

Samuel is a nurse, studying to be a Nurse Practitioner. He served two tours of duty in Iraq before he returned home an unemployed, thirty-year-old drunk. He was lonely and lost when he wandered into the Thrift Shop one day and found Sister Farkas having one of her spells. She has several different kinds of spells, but this was a fainting spell.

When she gave out a loud moan, as she always does, and slumped into a pile of hooded sweatshirts, Samuel ran to her aid. After that, Sr. Farkas took him under her wing. She listened to his painful war stories and somehow convinced him that her community was the answer to his needs.

Jane thinks Samuel is very handsome in a British Health Professional sort of way. He always stands perfectly straight and at almost six-feet is the tallest of the three ducks. His dark wavy hair falls loosely over his forehead, and his pale white skin looks shiny and scrubbed. All of the sisters secretly pray that he will become a priest.

"Sister Jane!" Samuel breaks ranks and sits her in a chair. "Look at these bandages, and your ankle is taped. Does this hurt?" He pushes gently on the bandage.

The third religious duck is Sister Mimi. *She's our youngest at twenty-nine and our shortest at five foot three.* Jane fills with pride. Mimi is slender with medium-length blonde hair and deep blue eyes that add to the attractiveness of her always-pleasant personality. She arrived from France eight months ago to learn modern methods of community management. These new techniques will be brought back and shared with her Sisters in France.

Mimi flips her hair away from her face, smiles compassionately, and gently pushes in front of the others to give Jane a warm hug. The hug is so enthusiastic it makes Jane wince.

Mimi recoils immediately. "Oh ma amie, poor, poor Jane. You are broken, yes?"

"I am broken, yes." Jane slips into a slight accent. "But they are only bruises."

"Just how did this happen, Jane?" Magdalene is brusque. "Are you all right?"

"I twisted my ankle in the middle of the street...a truck was coming...I was almost killed." Jane tries to abbreviate her explanation.

"Is it broken?" Samuel bends over to examine the ankle. "Did you break your ankle?"

"Oh no, zee angle!" Mimi clasps her hands together.

"It's not broken. I just twisted my angle...I mean ankle." Jane continues, "It's just swollen. I need to soak it."

Jane is addressing Mimi and a questioning look comes over the young Sister's face.

"Zoak eet? What eez zoak eet?"

"Soak it? Is that what the doctor said?" Samuel takes medical control over the situation. "You can't walk on it. We need crutches or a wheelchair." He quickly leaves in search of the needed equipment.

Magdalene never allows anyone else to take control. "You weren't crossing at the corner, by the light, were you Jane?" Magdalene fires her first accusation. Jane knows more are to come.

"You weren't thinking about what you were doing. You were careless, Jane. You could be dead right now with no thought of your responsibilities."

Samuel returns with a wheelchair. He unintentionally puts some pressure on Jane's side as he moves her, and she winces again. "What is it? Did you hurt your ribs, too?"

Jane gives a half-smile. Half of her is enjoying the attention; the other half is moved by this outward display of love surrounding her.

"When she pushed me out of the street," Jane tries to explain. "I hit the curb and bruised my ribs."

"Bluesed her reebs? Oh ma amie, Jane!" Mimi pauses. "What eez bluesed reebs?" Mimi is concerned and grammatically confused.

"B-r-u-i-s-e-d...r-i-b-s." This is Samuel's way of gently correcting Mimi's English. He is still looking at Jane when he adds, "You'll have to stay in bed and rest."

"What?" Magdalene never lets information pass unnoticed. She also thinks too much attention is a waste of time unless it motivates action. "Who pushed you out of the street?"

The ducks stand silently in a row waiting for the answer.

Jane measures each word. "A woman pushed me out of the way of a truck and saved my life. It was an act of God...I think. She almost got killed saving me. She hit her head and has amnesia. The authorities want to lock her up in jail or a mental hospital. I can't let that happen. She will be coming home with us until she is identified or recovers her memory."

Everyone remains silent except Magdalene. "Home with us?" She clears her throat. "I understand your feeling of obligation, Jane, and your dislike for the alternatives given to this woman. But do you really think this is a good idea? We know nothing about her. She may not be open to living in a convent."

Jane responds quickly. "An old house on a noisy city street hardly fits the preconceived idea of a convent, even if we call it that."

"We are not equipped for this kind of caretaking," Magdalene protests.

"We are very well-equipped. Samuel is a nurse; Mimi is a counselor; you are a retired teacher; and we have a spare bedroom. Most importantly, and I don't think I need to remind any of you of this, we are called as religious to help those who need our help. I have made up my mind, Magdalene. If she wants to come with us, she can."

"You mean you haven't asked her yet? Please, Jane, reconsider this latest..." Magdalene searches for a word, "Whim. Are you even thinking rationally?"

"This is not a *whim*, and I am being as rational as I always am."

Sister Amnesia
17

Jane ends any further discussion. "I'm going to see her now, to thank her, and to invite her to stay with us. You may wait for me in the waiting area."

Before she can get up, Samuel is on one side and Mimi on the other, practically lifting her into the wheelchair.

Jane takes control of the chair. "I'm not going very far. I'll be all right." She motions the three ducks to the Waiting Room and flags down a passing nurse who directs Jane to the cubicle where the woman with amnesia is waiting.

******

The mystery woman sits on a chair, fully dressed in black leather pants, leather boots, and now blood-stained leather jacket. Her face is puffy and pale with a large rectangular bandage over her forehead. She dejectedly stares at her hands. When Jane wheels herself in, the young woman looks at her and asks, "Can I go now? Can I leave?"

Jane feels the woman's desperation. She's familiar enough with fear to always feel its presence in a room. She smiles and tries to bring some calm to the situation. "I'm Jane Dalton." She holds out her hand. "I want to thank you for saving my life today. I'm very grateful. You were very brave."

The leather-clad woman takes her hand and stands up. She smiles back. "I was? I was brave? I wish I could remember that."

"You pushed me out of the way of a speeding truck. I could have been killed, but you saved my life." Jane smiles.

The young woman pushes against the bandage on her forehead. She can't stop the headache or psychic pain she feels. "I can't remember. I can't seem to remember anything." She touches her jacket and slacks. "I don't even remember these clothes."

She looks at Jane. "You know, you look kind of familiar. What's your name again?"

"It's Jane Dalton, Sister Jane Dalton."

"You're my sister! That's great!" The woman moves closer. "The doctor told me no one knew who I was. I was pretty scared."

Jane needs to correct the misunderstanding. "I'm not your sister, I'm a religious sister, a nun. Do you remember what a nun is?"

The woman presses her forehead again and distrust is evident in her tone. "Of course I do. What do you think, I'm stupid?" She backs away from Jane, trying to maintain her bravado. "I just hurt my head you know. I didn't lose my brains."

Jane sits quietly, not knowing what to say. The woman is thinking, shrewdly planning a protective next move.

"I'm a nun, too!" She moves closer to Jane again.

Jane stifles a spontaneous laugh. "And do you remember your name?"

"Yes." The woman's expression is now cheerful and relieved. "I'm...I'm Sister...I'm Sister Hershey Ghirardelli."

Jane can't help it. She starts to laugh. Tears roll down her face, and she tries to gain control, but she can't stop laughing. She clutches her sore ribs and holds them tightly. She finally stops when she sees the young woman's expression has changed back to somber and distrustful.

"I'm sorry...Hershey. I wasn't laughing at your...unusual name or at you. I mean, I think it's just a release of tension. I've been very upset by all that's happened today."

The young woman nods, her mind planning a different tact. "Well, maybe I'm not a nun." She sits down again and stares at her boots. She appears small and frightened.

"I don't want to stay in this hospital. I'm afraid. I can't remember things, and my mind has big black holes like these clothes. It's scary. Sometimes I close my eyes, and I think I can see all the way to the stars...outer space...planets...you know. I'm afraid they'll put me in some room and leave me there. I don't want to be left alone. I don't want to just float around in the darkness or in space."

She looks at Jane. "Please don't let them leave me here. I'm afraid. I just want to go where there are people. I want to be someone." Her voice begins to crack, and she stops talking.

Jane wheels closer. "I won't let them leave you here. I'd like you to come and stay with me, at least until someone comes for you or until you remember things."

The woman's voice is tired and sad. "I'm pretty sure I'm really Hershey Ghirardelli. That name is totally familiar."

Jane feels a bond she hasn't felt for years. She likes this woman. "All right then, you're Hershey Ghirardelli until we find out otherwise. Are you ready to leave?"

"I'm ready to get out of here." Hershey practically bounces to her feet. She grabs a plastic bag from the tray table and shakes it. "I guess these are all my things."

She holds it up to Jane. It contains a roll of money and the three earrings. "What do you think these things are?" She points to the earrings.

"Those are your earrings." Jane tries to be matter of fact.

Hershey looks closely at the bag. "My earrings?"

Jane takes advantage of this interest for some reality orientation. She takes the bag and puts the earrings and the chain into Hershey's hand. She points to the gun and cross and explains, "These are the two earrings you wore on your left ear."

"How...how did I wear them?" Hershey is an eager student.

"You have two holes in that ear. You can see them in the mirror." Jane points to a small mirror on the tray table. Hershey walks back and holds up the mirror. She looks at her ear and pokes at the two holes.

Jane tries to explain by holding up the earrings. "You put this post through that hole and put this on the back to hold it. The cross goes into the other hole."

Hershey grimaces. "Ooooh, who would do that? Put holes in their ears?" She pauses. "And where does the third one go?" She looks at her other ear which has no holes. Then she notices the small hole above her left nostril. Her voice gets softer. "In my nose. I have a hole in my nose, and I put an earring in that hole?"

Jane holds out the diamond and shows Hershey how the chain attaches to the earring.

"Do many nuns wear these?" Fortunately, Hershey is speaking to the mirror.

Jane stifles another laugh attack. "Not really. At least not many that I know or any that live in our house." She returns the bag to Hershey. "Which reminds me, there are three other religious who live in our house. I hope you will be patient with them. We don't get many visitors."

Jane motions for Hershey to follow, and she wheels out of the cubicle. She quietly calls for her waiting Sisters and Brother.

The three ducks stop and stare at Hershey. She stares back at them. After this awkward pause, each is introduced. Sister Mary Magdalene McDonald does not step forward. She smoothes out the wrinkles on her perfect A-line skirt and throws Jane a "This is not the type of person we take to our convent" look.

Jane returns the look with an "I am in charge and this is my decision" counter-look.

"Brother Samuel Deane and Sister Mimi...Miriam Fournier, I would like you both to meet..." Jane tries to lighten her tone to alleviate some of the tension. "This is Hershey Ghirardelli."

Samuel and Mimi step closer, and Hershey stiffly shakes their hands.

Mimi takes Jane's congeniality cue and asks, "Eet eez an Italian name, no?" Her friendly demeanor and strange question help break the awkwardness of this situation.

Samuel smiles and also tries to help. "Mimi thinks your name is Italian." He moves closer and directs an immediate medical concern to Hershey. "That looks like a nasty cut. Do you know how many stitches you got?" He touches Hershey's bandage, and she feels a sudden jolt of electricity radiate down her entire body.

"Do you have any pain in your jaw or your neck?" He asks as he touches her forehead again. Another jolt of pure warmth races down Hershey's nerve endings.

She blankly replies, "No."

"That's good." Samuel smiles and steps back into line.

Jane feels this is an opportune moment to suggest they all go home. Samuel promptly takes his position behind her wheelchair, and Mimi moves solicitously to her side. This forces Magdalene to walk next to Hershey. Magdalene straightens her shoulders and stares straight ahead. In one of her usual huffs, she sarcastically mumbles, "It is an odd name."

Hershey tries to keep pace with her and readily replies, "It's really Sister Hershey Ghirardelli. Does that sound better?"

Magdalene does not reply. She walks faster and catches up with Jane and the others. This leaves Hershey alone walking behind them.

CHAPTER 3

A small newspaper ad describes Hershey as a missing person. It asks anyone with knowledge of her to contact the paper or Sister Jane. It runs unanswered for three weeks.

A feature story about the accident with a photo of Jane and Hershey recuperating in the convent living room appears on the second front page of the local paper. No one calls, no one writes, and no one comes forward to claim Hershey.

The newspaper offers a discount to the Sisters if they wish to continue the ad. Jane discusses the cost effectiveness with the others and all, including Hershey, agree not to spend more money.

"It's just a matter of time until word gets around," Jane reassures Hershey. "Maybe someone who knows you has been out of town. When they get back and look for you, they'll find out about the amnesia." Hershey accepts this with obvious skepticism. Unfortunately, that's also the spirit in which it's given.

Mimi decides to take Hershey under her generous and giving wing. "Chère Jane, I wish to use my skeels to help Hershey adjust to our strange world."

"I wouldn't use the word, 'strange'." Jane cautions. "Especially in front of Magdalene. But you're right. It isn't a world that Hershey is likely to be familiar with, not with those leather clothes and her haircut."

"I think she has bean sent to us." Mimi shares a prophesy. "I think she wheel help us do good for God."

Jane tries to believe what Mimi says but her injuries are more debilitating than expected. Her convalescence has given her too much time to examine her past. She avoids this whenever possible. She doesn't like climbing the mountain of reflection, and she rejects the idea of pulling out the past and examining it in order to put it to rest. Her life moves laterally not vertically.

"I don't mind giving up anger, Lord, but I don't want fear," Jane prays. "I really was on my way to that counseling center. I took the first step, but I twisted my ankle. The accident seems to be pulling me into a new direction, but I feel an overwhelming foreboding. Please, make your will known?"

Jane is preparing for the Annual Assembly of all Sisters of St. Francis Dupre which will be held in Iowa in less than two months. The Syracuse Sisters will travel to the Midwest with other Sisters from the Eastern United States. The entire community will come together to reaffirm the meaning of their vows and the mission of their order which is to help all outsiders in our world.

Jane is writing her opening speech. "All of the religious orders in America have declined. There are only a handful of Sisters of St. Francis left in Syracuse, and it is sometimes difficult to see how we are making a difference in the world. However, when hundreds of us gather to share our new programs, a great sense of accomplishment and belonging emerges."

Mimi has cheerfully claimed the kitchen since her arrival. No one fights to replace her since cooking on a limited budget is tedious and frustrating. But Mimi finds cooking exhilarating and challenging. Jane assumes this is a French thing and just thanks God for providing.

Mimi hums as she struggles with the translation of recipes. She has welcomed Hershey into her kitchen as an apparent protégé. Mimi sees it as an opportunity to discuss daily living skills and propriety in appearance. A request is made to visit the Thrift Shop for some suitable clothing for Hershey.

Jane gives her permission but insists that Samuel accompany the two women. He is familiar with the store and the dangers of the surrounding neighborhood.

******

Mimi pulls into an empty parking spot right in front of the Thrift Shop. Samuel slides out of the passenger seat and carefully checks out the empty street. He holds the door open for Hershey and again glances around this economically depressed area. The Thrift Shop is the only occupied storefront on the block. Across the street is an old tavern called O'Hoolihans. Two regulars in their dark trousers and faded shirts wait for the bar to open.

"Stay alert," Samuel reminds Mimi. "It's not always this quiet around here." He tries to explain to Hershey. "In another hour, the guys from the sheet metal factory will be down here for the O'Hoolihans' lunch special."

He helps Hershey out of the back seat, and she inquisitively asks, "What's the lunch special?"

Samuel laughs. "It's not very special, baloney on white bread and American cheese with butter. Most of those guys don't come for the sandwiches. They come for the dark Irish ale. That's the *real* lunch special."

Mimi leads the group into the store and adds, "Our Sister Farkas eez ninety-three, and she says zee ale is good for zee constitution."

Hershey enters expecting to be greeted by an ancient, perhaps feeble nun. Instead, a busy and spry Sister Farkas gives them a big wave. She is finishing a sale with a needy Sudanese immigrant. Sister Farkas cheerily adds two free boxes of cereal and a jug of laundry soap to the grateful customer's packages.

Mimi crosses the overrun room festooned with tables of all sizes, piled high with clothing, shoes, toys, dishes, and assorted household supplies. She reaches Sister Farkas who gives her a big hug. "Bonjour, my little Mimi."

Mimi smiles. "Bonjour chère Farkas."

"We don't like to sneak up on Sister Farkas," Samuel whispers to Hershey. "And she doesn't like us to just pop in unannounced. She says it doesn't give her time to tidy up."

He shrugs and smiles. Their eyes seem to lock onto each other until Hershey looks away. "She doesn't look in her nineties, but I suppose she doesn't like surprises anymore."

Samuel also pulls his attention back to Sister Farkas. "She just retired from nursing ten years ago. She told me the nursing home where she worked was getting too indifferent to the patients. Since she couldn't change the nursing home, she could change herself. She helped open the Thrift Shop. She has so much compassion for people."

Sister Farkas marches up to him. "How's my favorite nurse?" The five-foot tall Farkas looks up but doesn't wait for an answer. "Did you finally take time off from that studying to come and visit me?"

She laughs at her own sense of humor and gives Samuel a healthy punch on the arm. Then she turns to Hershey. "This must be the new mystery Sister living at your convent." She carefully studies Hershey's multi-colored, shaggy hair and leather outfit. Then she spontaneously wraps her short arms around Hershey and hugs her too.

"I'm Sister Farkas LaMont. I run this shop. But I served God faithfully as a nurse for sixty-years. My father always said...you may have heard of my father, Barrymore LaMont. He performed on Broadway in the early twenties. Anyway, as Daddy always said, 'Don't get stuck in just one job, diversify your talents.' That's what I'm doing now. So, how can I help you? What brings all of you to the Shop?"

"Chère Farkas." Mimi explains their mission. "Chère Hershey has no suitable clothing. We come to help her feel her closet."

Farkas looks at Hershey again. "I don't suppose these leather duds are going over too big with Jane and Magdalene." She thinks of Magdalene's unwavering sense of decorum and chuckles. "I'm surprised you lasted this long with Magdalene."

Mimi tries to help. "Chère Hershey sometimes borrows clothing from me or Sister Jane, but eet does not feet so good."

Farkas leads the group behind the counter, through the curtained doorway, and into a back room. This room is as vast as the front. One side is filled with furniture and the other side holds bags and bags of unsorted clothing. To the far left are several racks set off from the rest.

She goes right to the racks. "This is where I put any clothing suitable for our Sisters…and Sam. Let me see…" She takes a grey blazer, similar to the one Samuel is wearing and holds it up to Hershey. "Why not try this on?"

She pushes through the clothes on another rack and comes back with an almost matching grey skirt. Hershey holds it up next to the blazer, and Farkas nods approvingly. This search and find routine goes on for another fifteen minutes. Hershey now holds two suits, a grey one and a navy one, several white blouses, a cream-colored blouse, and a pair of grey slacks.

Farkas and Mimi do a last check of the sizes and then ask the fashionably confused Hershey to hold up each selection for proper length. This gives Samuel a chance to return to the front of the store and hunt for some jeans. He moves to another table and rummages around for several tee shirts. He bags the clothes and returns to the clothing metamorphosis happening in the back room.

Hershey emerges from the dressing room wearing a grey skirt, a white blouse with all the buttons buttoned, and a grey blazer. Her face shows sheer exhaustion. Nurse Samuel takes over. "I think Hershey has done enough shopping for today. Remember, she isn't completely recovered from her head injury."

This is enough of a hint for Farkas. "Oh, you poor thing." She pats Hershey's arm. "I think you look lovely. I'll just bag the rest, and you can go home and rest."

Farkas bags the new clothes and looks at her watch. "It's almost noon, and Thursday is my day with the boys at O'Hoolihans. Hate to rush you out, but I only get an hour for lunch."

She ends their visit with a quick hug to Mimi, Hershey, and Samuel, who gets an extra punch on the arm. Farkas locks the store and heads for O'Hoolihans, while Mimi, who is very proud of her International Driver's License, unlocks the car and gets behind the wheel.

Hershey slides into the back and sinks into the seat. She is surrounded by bags of neutral-colored clothing. Samuel turns to Hershey and hands her the bag of jeans and tee shirts. She gives him a quizzical look.

"Just a few things to wear when you want to relax," he explains. "They may feel more familiar than the clothes you just got. I hope you like them." He gives Hershey a shy smile and turns back.

"Thanks. Thank you...Samuel." Hershey checks out the bag.

"I know what it feels like to not fit in." Samuel tries to explain as he stares out the front window. "When I came back from Iraq, I was different. I had changed. I didn't fit in anywhere. I tried to go home, but I wasn't like my brothers anymore. It was hunting season. I didn't want to go out and kill anymore. And my Mom just stayed awake all night checking on me. She was looking for her son, but he didn't come home. I couldn't even take off my uniform for months. It had my name on it, and I wasn't anyone without it. I didn't seem to belong anywhere. Alcohol helped the pain but that didn't feel like home either.

He looks at Mimi who gives him a smile. "The Sisters taught me a different kind of following orders." He goes on. "They call it obedience, but not just following the will of God or a Superior's request. They taught me to remember my obedience to self, to be who I really am, at least sometimes. It adds the balance that God wants for us. I think that means I need to dress down a little. You know, sometimes feel like my clothes really fit me.

He turns back to Hershey. "I think the clothes in that bag look like they might really fit you when you need to dress down.

******

It's another day in Mimi's kitchen, and she is explaining to Hershey the necessity of a good image. "We are zee Christian women and zee Catholic Church. We are to be modest and pure in our clothing. Blouzes or a plain suit or dress eez proper...not zee black leather."

Mimi does defer to Hershey wearing socks instead of stockings, since Hershey's high black boots are cheaper than investing in new shoes. This is Mimi's only concession. "No matter eef we are not in zee habit, we are zee symbol of God's purity."

Jane listens approvingly from her office, and she hears Hershey's response. "Do you really think God only wears navy blue and grey?"

Jane stifles her laugh, so she can hear Mimi answer. "I do not really know, I tell you only what I have bean told. Eet seems, eef She wears anything, eet eez zee skirt."

The reference to God as feminine is followed by mutual laughter, including Jane's. She loves a joyful house and prays that Hershey is getting the attention she is missing from those who really know and love her.

The sisters' vow of poverty is taken seriously. They share what they have which isn't much. Everything is donated, second hand, or inexpensive. Nothing is wasted, including Hershey's two hundred dollars, which is immediately put into the locked tackle box in the office. Any use of this money will involve the consent of everyone in the house.

Food is plentiful but confusing to Hershey who only remembers hamburgers, French fries, and cola. None of which appears in the convent. She helps Mimi with the cooking, but religious meals are all new to her. On one of her training days, Mimi announces, "Today, we make zee 'Zerimp Zurprise'."

Hershey remembers something. "Shrimp! I love shrimp! I used to eat it all the time. Shrimp cocktail with hot sauce, deep fried shrimp with slaw or baked shrimp with all that butter."

A small memory creeps into the corner of her mind. "Mimi, I remember something! I think I used to eat shrimp on a big bus, but it wasn't a regular bus. It was like a living room in the back of a bus with a refrigerator full of shrimp."

"That eez good, very good!" Mimi is always encouraging. "Chère Hershey, zee memory maybe comes back. Zee bus maybe eez a zymbol, a motor home, or just a bus, so cooking eez good. But zee zerimp zurprise, eet has no zerimp, that eez zee zurprise."

Hershey is quick to adjust and becomes fond of vegetables au jus. What she remembers about her old food is lost in this new experience. She is gaining confidence and losing some of her fear. Her innate intelligence is apparent especially during theological reflections and discussions.

Jane is confused by what she perceives in Hershey's intellect and abilities, and what she remembers of Hershey's initial appearance. Perhaps the clue to who Hershey really is does not lie in her clothing but in her being.

Jane and Hershey meet weekly for Directed Study time. More often than not, Hershey gets depressed. She presses her hand against her forehead. "I'm afraid sometimes. I just can't remember. It's like a blackness in my mind, a darkness that I can't even pray away."

Jane tries to help. "Don't worry. You'll be fine and remember everything...very soon. When you least expect it, something will trigger your memory, and all your old life will come back to you."

Jane tries to help the only way she knows how, by teaching Hershey new ways of praying. This is done out of the range of Magdalene, who thinks Jane is toying with psychic mumbo jumbo. Hershey is an eager student, something Jane loves. These lessons are a reminder of her own journey of faith. She often wonders if Hershey, in a past life, was perhaps some kind of eccentric nun.

But this idea is put in doubt during evening prayers when Hershey insists on singing the refrain in a loud rhythm and blues style. Magdalene suggests rather adamantly that Hershey spend at least some time each week practicing liturgical singing with Samuel, who is very good at chanting responses.

Jane thinks keeping Hershey busy is practical and agrees, but Samuel nervously begs off the assignment. He has a full schedule of work and study. Mimi happily volunteers and the rhythm and blues end except on special occasions when nothing can stop Hershey from musically rejoicing. Jane rather likes these occasions.

Then there is the issue of sex. Jane always feared the subject of sex might come up. She's never comfortable discussing sex and never met a nun who was, except Mimi.

"Zex eez most natural." Mimi is answering a question Jane didn't hear. "Eet eez how we responds to zee...what eez zee word? Movements...no, no...urgements...no, no... zee zex feelings. Eet eez how we respond to zee feelings that make Sisters different."

"How do we respond?" Hershey can always be depended on for the next question.

"I do not think about eet. I try to keep with activity." Mimi rattles pans, trying not to think of "eet."

"What if you get...you know...frisky...randy... horny?" Hershey seems to have a vast vocabulary of slang.

"Orny?" Mimi does not know the word.

Hershey hunts for a synonym. "Horny...worked up...sexy...turned on. Don't you ever get turned on? Like when you see a picture or hear some music or something?"

The pans rattle louder and then abruptly stop. "We are only human. I also am with feelings. Eef they come, I let them go. You wheel see, chère Hershey. Zex becomes of very little concern after a time. I get zee orny from prayer now."

"No, Mimi!" Hershey knows this is not a good use of this new vocabulary word. "You can't say you get horny from prayer."

"But why? I do get zee feelings to do good and build up zee kingdom."

"That's not horny. That's maybe worked up but not horny. Please don't tell anyone you get horny over prayers, okay?"

"Okay, chère Hershey. I wheel not use zee new word. I wheel not be orny over anything. But you must speak of zex to Jane. She wheel answer you better than I. Eet eez a subject she wheel know better."

That is one of the problems of being Moderator of the house. Sex is not a subject Jane knows better than Mimi, but the only other choice is Magdalene. What would she say to Hershey? "We don't think about it! We don't talk about it! It doesn't exist!"

Jane wonders if she can do any better. Part of her thinks Magdalene's advice is true for some at a certain age but probably not at Hershey's age. Jane will give "it" some thought before Hershey brings up the question.

*****

Hershey unintentionally shakes up the entire house. The Sisters' and Brother's secure existence is being intruded upon by unfamiliar noise. Hershey plays popular stations on the radio...rather loudly, and she asks questions that no one has ever asked or thought about since before they joined the community.

Magdalene hates loudness and only speaks in a controlled whisper. She knows what a sister should be, and it is not Hershey. Magdalene reiterates her concern to Jane. "A *Sister* does not wear boots and pink hair. A *Sister* does not speak loudly or make noise. And when told to clean the bathrooms, a *Sister* does not say, 'When is it your turn?'"

Magdalene takes a breath before continuing. "A *Sister* is always modest and reserved. A *Sister* does not belch even if she then excuses herself. *She* does not wear her pajamas outside of her bedroom even with a robe which Hershey does not own. Moreover, *Sisters* do not lay across the parlor couch with bare feet even if no one else is sitting there."

Magdalene tries to avoid Hershey. When they're forced together at meals, she just corrects Hershey's manners or use of utensils. Jane reminds Magdalene that it is a sin to crush a person's spirit. Still, Magdalene finds Hershey insufferable. Hershey is a reminder of all the students she never liked, the lazy, boisterous, wasters-of-time and effort, her effort.

Magdalene cannot help herself. This Hershey person does not belong in her private little world. Hershey is an intruder, an interloper, a divisive force. Certainly Jane can look at Samuel, even Mimi with her cultural anomalies, and see how different they are from this Hershey.

Why doesn't Jane do something about it? Magdalene mentally demands. *Until Jane does, I will have to pray for patience.* This doesn't prove to be easy.

CHAPTER 4

Agent Whittington takes off his sunglasses and reaches into his pocket for his vibrating cell phone. He flips open the phone as he looks out the plane window. The highway below is lined with cars and trucks scurrying home like ants to their hill. "I got Anastasia's report and no, it isn't that helpful. I think she's losing her touch." He listens. "So the old woman is a nun, so what?"

He brushes a piece of lint off his pants. "Now that is helpful because we know there's a connection. There was an American nun over there at the time of the sighting. I'm on my way to Syracuse, New York to have a little talk with her."

He checks through some papers on his lap. "Her name is Jane Dalton, Sister Jane Dalton. My gut tells me she has information we need. And I'm going to get that information."

******

On a typically quiet Sunday evening, everyone but Hershey is sitting on the second-hand maroon velour sofa and matching chair in the convent parlor with the maroon flowered wallpaper. Jane is ensconced in the sagging-springs of the matching chair doing needlework. Mimi sits on the sofa across from her and winds various colored yarns into balls. Magdalene and Samuel are at the other end of the sofa watching the video, "Praying as St. Nugent Prayed."

Hershey has gone to shower and change into her pajamas. Jane knows that Hershey is waiting for the video tape to end and everyone to retire. This is when she sneaks back into the parlor to watch the late-night movie.

Hershey's bedroom is across from Jane's and next to Magdalene's room, just down the hall from the parlor. The other two bedrooms and the Chapel are upstairs.

Jane is a light sleeper, almost an insomniac, a burden she carries from her past. She has caught Hershey watching the late-night movies several times. "These movies help me fall asleep." Hershey tried to explain. "I think they work better than those night prayers." Then she looked wistfully at the television screen. "Do you think maybe I was a movie star? Some of these flix look so familiar."

Jane tried to be tactful. "Someone would have recognized you by now, if you were a movie star."

She tried to keep Hershey company for a few nights but quickly realized that evening prayers worked better for her. Jane prefers sleeplessness in the privacy of her own room.

This particular Sunday is no different than all the others to Jane. She's grateful for the security of standard routines. She smiles at the rapt attention both Samuel and Magdalene give to the video. Mimi, who is now knitting, is equally absorbed in listening to the message of St. Nugent.

However, this Sunday's studied silence is suddenly broken by Hershey's screaming entrance from the bathroom. She rushes into the parlor clutching a short hand towel to her chest. "Jane! Jane! Look at this! I never noticed it before! I looked in the mirror...and look at this!"

She's now standing in front of them with all eyes on her mostly uncovered body. She blocks the television as she twirls around to reveal her bare backside. She is excitedly unaware that she is mooning her conservative Sisters and Brother.

"I think I remember something!" She yells over her shoulder.

All eyes focus on Hershey's left gluteus maximus. Covering this entire muscular area is an ornate tattoo of a blue dragon with a long, fiery red tongue.

"Do we have any Chinese Sisters? I remember a Chinese Sister. I think her name is Manchu, Sister Manchu." Hershey excitedly goes on.

Magdalene is first to shake free of their hypnotic posterior trance. She shoots up out of her chair. "Jane, this is too much! It is irreverent and unbecoming to our station!" She storms past Hershey and out of the room.

Jane expects Samuel to follow, but he doesn't. He does close his mouth which fell open on Hershey's entrance.

Jane is a little overcome by such a spirited and unfamiliar entrance, but she addresses Hershey quietly and calmly. "I'm afraid, we don't have any Chinese Sisters. Perhaps the tattoo means something else?"

The full reality of her amnesia hits Hershey. Her face, so hopeful and animated, falls into deep disappointment. She turns around to face Jane again, and the small towel hangs in a vertical defeated stripe that hardly covers anything.

"Perhaps you should go and get dressed." Jane isn't sure of what else to say. Hershey's visible disappointment overshadows any reprimand Jane might have in mind. Actually, she doesn't have any in mind.

"I was sure the tattoo meant something. When I saw it in the mirror, I was sure." Hershey's voice is now tired and beaten. "Why would I remember that name? Does everyone have one of these?" She half turns once again to point out the artistic gluteus.

"Not that I'm aware of." Jane can feel the eyes in the room turn to her. "It's chilly in here. I wouldn't want you to catch a cold."

This again is all Jane can think of to say. It's enough. Hershey moves slowly back to the bathroom, looking much like a sculpture entitled, "Nude Walking Dejectedly Away."

"We need to talk when you're dressed," Jane calls after her. "I'll come to your room."

Mimi and Samuel have returned to their projects. Mimi is knitting, Samuel is watching the video. Jane tries to finish the stitch she started before Hershey's entrance. No one speaks.

Mimi finally breaks the thick silence. "I believe eet eez zee scorpion, an oriental scorpion."

Jane looks up, but Mimi keeps knitting. Jane's face begins to form an involuntary smile.

Samuel's gaze is glued to the television. "That's not a scorpion." He continues reading the end credits. "It's a dragon, a blue dragon with a red tongue."

Jane is stifling a laugh. She quickly puts her needlework away and gets ready to leave the room. The two other members of her house are not afraid to acknowledge what has just happened, so why should she be afraid? "I'm going to have a talk with Hershey."

Mimi can't contain herself any more. She looks at Jane and they both start to laugh. Samuel puts his face into his hands and almost smothers trying to suppress his laughter. This sets the other two off again and the room resounds with laughter.

Jane regains her composure and leaves the other two who are still giggling. She pauses for a moment at Hershey's door. The momentary humor of this situation is a stark contrast to Hershey's anguish at the loss of another clue to her identity. Jane prays for wisdom and an open heart. She'll need these qualities to help her new friend.

She knocks. "May I come in?"

Hershey opens the door and moves to the end of her single bed. Her face is red and puffy. She stares at the floor.

Jane closes the door and sits next to Hershey. "Are you all right?"

Hershey looks up. "I thought the tattoo was important. I just thought someone would recognize it. I feel so different from everyone else. I feel out of place. I feel so lost."

She leans into Jane and starts to cry. Jane puts her arm around Hershey and tries to smooth the stubble of multi-colored hair that's beginning to grow in. "You are a little different from everyone here." Jane says softly.

Hershey composes herself, and Jane tries some humor. "To my knowledge, none of the Sisters here have tattoos. Actually, I'm not sure any of the Sisters here have bodies. You may not have noticed, but most of us are rather shy about certain things, especially nudity."

Hershey's expression now reveals a shocking awareness of what she has just done. "I didn't have any clothes on! I never thought, Jane! I'm sorry. I just never thought. That's why Magdalene got so upset. I was just thinking of the tattoo. I never thought about the clothes."

Jane gives her a smile. "Don't worry Hershey. I think it's good for us once in awhile. We tend to forget our human side. We all need to come face to face with our bodies from time to time."

Hershey begins to relax. "Face to face...but that wasn't my face. I'm so embarrassed! I just showed my ass to everyone in this house and all for nothing. I must be losing my mind, not just my memory but my whole mind."

Jane shakes her head. "There's nothing wrong with your mind. Running into the parlor was just a spontaneous thing, and I think we did find another clue to who you are." She takes Hershey's hand. "You're not crazy, Hershey. Don't ever think that or let anyone else try to make you think that. Your memory will return. The doctor said it could come back at any time. I'm very sure it will."

Hershey slowly pulls back her hand. "I just want to know who I am. I feel okay here, but I know I have a past. I know I had a different life with different people. It's frustrating and a little scary. I find clues that seem to jog my memory, but then it just goes empty again. I want to belong somewhere…be a part of some whole, not just a visitor. I feel so lonely all the time, so out of place."

Jane stands. "As Moderator of this house, I may need to remind you more often that you need to try and fit in a little more. Ask questions if you don't understand something. Answers might help you feel less lost. You're one of us for now, and I'd like you to feel that you belong. That you are a Sister just like Samuel is a brother.

"Hold onto your faith, Hershey. When that darkness starts to come over you, remember what's really important. Try to be with God in love, that's all that really matters. I know having faith is hard, and I really do understand what you're feeling." She walks toward the door. "Good night."

******

Jane closes Hershey's door and crosses to her own room. She's about to open her door when Magdalene touches her arm. "Jane, this is the last straw!"

"I know the nudity was upsetting for you, Magdalene." Jane tries to be reassuring. "Hershey was just excited. She didn't think about the effect of her appearance on you and the others. She was sure the tattoo was a clue to her identity. She's not yet aware of our ways."

Magdalene is cold. "She's not going to get used to our ways. She obviously does not belong here. I'm not sure where she does belong, but I know it is not here. She must leave as quickly as possible. I told you it was a mistake to bring her here, and I think tonight proves your decision was wrong. I think she should leave tomorrow."

Magdalene's unbending attitude is what keeps Jane praying for an open heart. She doesn't want to be what Magdalene is becoming. She doesn't want to be so afraid of change and differences. Magdalene has become so afraid of the tactile essences in life that she has stopped feeling anything but the familiar. And sometimes her familiar is cold and negative. Every time Jane opens the gates of her heart to Maggie, an incident occurs, and Maggie manages to slam the gate closed again.

"Hershey's staying!" Jane forcefully announces. "Whether you like her being here or not, whether her presence riles your sense of righteousness or not, whether she's your idea of a Sister or not. She's staying!"

"I'm sorry you feel that way, Jane. I was afraid you would." Magdalene is too calm, too controlled. "I called Mother General in Iowa. I told her you aren't feeling well again. I told her, I will take over your duties."

Jane's anger starts at her feet and slowly floods up to her neck. She can feel her entire body stiffen and her breathing almost stop. She doesn't raise her voice. Instead, she punctuates every word. "You had no right to do that. The phone call and offer are very inappropriate and quite unnecessary."

"I found the call very necessary." Magdalene has already rehearsed her comments. "You put all of us in danger especially our young Sister and Brother."

Jane cuts her off. "No one is in danger. For that matter, no one in this house is young. Who do you think you are? There's nothing wrong with me or my judgment and there never was. I thought we were clear on that. I thought you understood. I explained everything that happened in my past. Just why are you doing this, Magdalene? Is it the power? Is it the control? Then for goodness sakes take it. I never wanted to be the Local Moderator. They elected me. This job was not my choice."

Magdalene remains unmoved. She gains strength from Jane's discomfort. "They didn't know about the hospitalization. None of the Sisters who voted knew about that. I tried to tell Mother General your election would be a mistake, but she wouldn't listen. She thought the position would help you, but I told her it was too much pressure."

Jane cuts her off. "I don't want to discuss this anymore. I'm not stepping down until I go to Iowa and talk to Mother General...I mean Claire, myself. If Claire asks me to remove myself from leadership, I will."

Jane takes a long hard look at Magdalene. "If she does remove me from this position, I will also consider leaving this house and living with some of our other Sisters. In the meantime, Hershey stays, so get used to her or leave early for the gathering in Iowa."

With this, Jane steps into her room and slams the door. *The past never really rests.* Painful memories, accusations and guilt come flooding back to her. Sometimes she thinks amnesia would be a blessing. Forgetting must certainly be easier. She lights her private altar candle and prays. She stares into the flame until no thoughts exist. Only the light fills her mind, a warm, bright, endless globe of energy. Her body and mind begin to relax. She becomes one with the light. She lets her past and future slip away. Now maybe she can sleep.

CHAPTER 5

Jane awakes well rested and buoyant. She joins the others for morning prayers and does not look at Magdalene. Nor does she pray for forgiveness. Anger feels like a good motivator, so she prays for courage to return to the community clinic for an appointment. She wants to examine her painful memories but facing therapy is still frightening. Perhaps the fight with Magdalene is forcing her to seek counsel in order to find peace.

Breakfast is abnormally quiet. Jane assumes everyone heard at least part of the argument or the slamming of her bedroom door. If they didn't, Magdalene's elaborate Morning Prayer concerning discernment and obedience should have tipped them off that something was wrong. No one even comments on Mimi's latest creation, "The Eggs St. Louie."

******

Magdalene, Mimi, and Samuel are not at home, and Hershey is in her room. Jane has been occupied for several hours with the financial record-keeping of her local community. She is mathematically relieved when the back doorbell rings. She hurries down the three steps to the entranceway and opens the door to a tall, slender, thirtyish-looking man with extremely shiny shoes. He smiles at her.

"I'm looking for Sister Jane Dalton." His voice is as well-manicured as his appearance.

"I'm Sister Jane." She extends her hand. "And you are…?"

He gives her a superficial shake and reaches into his inside jacket pocket. He snaps open his badge and photo ID. "I'm Agent Edward Whittington, FBI."

Jane leans in to read the ID with her bifocals, but before she can focus, he flips the ID closed and puts it back into his tailored suit pocket. "I need to ask you some questions, Sister. May I come in?"

Jane is genuinely excited. "The FBI, please come in! Prayers are being answered! I'm hoping this is about Hershey's identity." She escorts Agent Whittington to her office.

"I think I should get Hershey," she says. "Please sit down. She'll be so excited." She motions to the chair next to her desk and rushes to Hershey's bedroom.

"Hershey, you must come to the office." Jane is almost breathless. "Someone from the FBI has come with news about your identity."

Hershey shoots out of her room, moves in front of Jane, and leads them both back to the office. Agent Whittington stands at attention for their entrance and holds out his hand to Hershey. "I'm Agent Edward Whittington, FBI."

Jane thinks he appears rather robot-like but quickly chastises herself. He is about to deliver some long-awaited good news.

Hershey is not as excited as Jane. She's more restrained, more suspicious. She lifts her hand slowly and sizes him up from his hair to his very shiny shoes.

"I'm…," she pauses. "I'm Sister Hershey Ghirardelli." She gives him a firm, strong handshake.

He just nods and waits for the women to sit before he does. Jane gets right to the point. "We've been waiting for some news for weeks now. What have you found out?"

Whittington looks puzzled. "You must have me confused with

someone else. I'm here about your suitcase. The one you lost on your trip to France."

"My suitcase." Jane is immediately disappointed. "I thought you were here with some news about Hershey. I forgot about my suitcase. Anyway, the suitcase was returned. The airlines delivered it to me several weeks ago."

The agent drops his composure for just a moment. Hershey takes special note of that moment. She watches him intently throughout the interview. He tries to ignore her and address his questions to Jane. "I don't know anything about Sister Hershey, but if you'd like me to check out something, I'd be glad to. My reason for this visit is the suitcase. Something has developed since the suitcase was recovered. We thought at first it was just a simple robbery."

He nervously catches Hershey staring at him. "It seems your suitcase was taken by some international drug smugglers. We have reason to believe that something very valuable and/or illegal is hidden in your bag. I'd like to take it back to our headquarters. It's very important for us to find the missing...."

He searches for the right word. "We need to recover evidence that can be used in our fight against these drug smugglers."

Jane is let down and somewhat skeptical of this whole story. "I didn't find anything missing or anything new in the suitcase. I think everything was checked by the police or customs before it was returned to me."

"That's true." He prepares another long explanation. "We have reason to believe that something is hidden in some part of the suitcase not in the contents. Can I have the suitcase, Sister?"

"That sounds more like an order than a request," Hershey answers for Jane.

Agent Whittington shoots another look at Hershey. "I didn't mean it to sound that way, but I want to impress on both of you how important this is to international security. Certainly you realize that stopping drug smuggling is a high priority for our President."

"Bull crap." Hershey slides into slang and sits up perfectly straight. "Why do you want the suitcase?"

Jane's eyebrows go up, but she lets Hershey continue. Little electric danger signals are running up and down her arms. She can't sit still. She's uncomfortable with this conversation, uncomfortable with this man.

Agent Whittington looks to Jane for assistance but none is forthcoming. "We want the suitcase. Either you give it to me now, or I'll get a search warrant and come back with a house-full of police. Which do you want?"

Hershey stands up. "What's in the suitcase?"

Whittington is angry now. His face is getting blotchy red spots and his meticulous manners are disintegrating. "It's none of your damn business, Sister...Amnesia. Just keep out of it, or you might find that no one is cooperating on that search for who you are."

This last comment jolts Jane back into action. "You do know about Hershey. Why didn't you say so? I don't know what's really going on but there's no need for trouble. I'll get the suitcase." She gets up.

Hershey jumps next to her. "I don't think you should give him anything until you find out what this is all about."

Whittington speaks directly to Hershey. "I told you this is none of your business. I'm warning you, I can have you thrown in jail for interfering in an investigation."

"Don't threaten me!" Hershey raises her voice. "I'm not afraid of you. And anyway, I'm not so sure you are FBI. I'd like to see some identification. Maybe I should call the FBI office? You don't mind if I check up on you, do you?"

He's rattled now. "I don't have to show you anything. I'm warning you, stay out of this!"

Jane is afraid. This last warning puts that knot back into her stomach. "Hershey, it's all right." Jane touches Hershey's arm. "I saw his identification, and I'll get the suitcase. You can come with me. I'll need some help. Mr. Whittington, please wait here."

She practically drags Hershey down to the basement. "Everything is all right." She tries to be reassuring. "It's only a suitcase, and I don't want any trouble especially for you."

Hershey reluctantly drags the large, faux-leather bag up the stairs. Whittington is waiting at the top of the stairs where Hershey hands it to him. He brushes past both of them and leaves by the back door.

"I don't like this." Hershey looks out the window at Whittington's car. "I don't like this at all, and I don't think he's FBI."

Jane peers out the window too. "Why don't you think he's FBI? And what don't you like about this?"

Hershey takes a glass from the cupboard. "I'm not sure. It's just a feeling." She runs the water for a minute and fills her glass.

"Is this feeling related to who you are?" Jane asks.

Hershey puts the glass down. "Maybe, maybe it is." She closes her eyes and rubs her forehead. "I keep hearing the words to a song. They're kinda funny really, but I keep hearing them play in my head ever since you introduced me to Whittington."

Jane moves to the old enamel-topped kitchen table and sits down. "What is the song, Hershey?"

Hershey sits across from her. "Did you ever hear the song, '*Oh My! Call the FBI*'?"

Jane didn't expect *Ave Maria*, but she didn't expect this either. "I can't say I'm familiar with that one, but I don't listen to much radio."

"I know it sounds weird, but I think Whittington is suspicious." Hershey speaks with a new urgency. "We really should check his credentials. I think this whole suitcase thing just isn't right. I mean, he's so mysterious and even rude. I don't trust him. Do you? Do you think he's telling the truth? And if he knows something about me, why doesn't he tell me?"

Jane lets her own thoughts replay the interview. "You're right! I'm going to call the FBI and find out just who he is." She heads back to the office.

Hershey isn't as quick as Jane and bumps her knee on the wooden table leg. She reaches the office just in time to see Jane push the green button on the phone.

"Hello, this is Sister Jane Dalton. I'd like to speak to someone in charge please. Yes, it's about a recent visit by someone who said he was an FBI agent." She holds for a moment and partially repeats her message. "Yes, this is Sister Jane Dalton. A man named Edward Whittington just came to our convent and said he was an FBI agent. He said he was looking for drugs in a suitcase I lost on my trip home from Europe."

She listens for a few minutes. "Hmm, yes, I see. Yes, I would appreciate that. Thank you. Goodbye."

Hershey sits up, blue eyes wide in anticipation. "Well? What did he say?"

Jane puts the phone down. "He said there is no agent named Edward Whittington in this area. He'll check with the national office but thinks it was a scam artist. If he doesn't find a Whittington, he'll send the local police over, and we can fill out a robbery report."

Hershey takes a long breath. "Wow! He's not with the FBI."

Jane shakes her head. "What would anyone want with my old suitcase? I don't think there's much of a market for torn and dented luggage."

"Has to be something in the suitcase," Hershey comments. "What was in it?"

"That's just the point." Jane tries to understand. "I went to France for a very short time. It was a courtesy trip. Mimi's house was having a symposium and asked if I could present a talk about our Clothing for the Poor Project. I was only there four days and never left the house, except for one dinner in a restaurant. That's where I met Magdalene's nephew, Sean and his wife, Shakeeta. It was on my last evening there."

Hershey crouches down, eye to eye with Jane. "So, what was in your suitcase?"

"I carried some clothes, two suits, pajamas, robe, and underwear." Jane taps her finger on her thigh. "On the way home, I packed my clothes, a magazine from the airplane, a box of chocolate truffles for Magdalene from their Moderator, Sister Vivienne, and a smoked fish."

She looks up and feels she must explain. "The French have a special way of smoking fish, and Magdalene is so fond of it. The fish wasn't really very big. It was in a plastic bag." She holds her hands about eight inches apart to illustrate the size.

Hershey wrinkles her face. "Are you sure that's all you had? What about souvenirs, medicine, or important papers? Anything else?"

Jane stares at the diamond pattern in the rug. "I did have the papers with my notes for the presentation and some slides of the people at our thrift store, some pictures Sean sent for Magdalene, and a few bottles of over-the-counter drugs."

She looks up again. "I carry a few prescriptions with me, but customs checked everything when I arrived in France and again when I returned. They were very thorough. There had been a bomb scare at the airport, so they checked everything very carefully."

Hershey paces the room. She stops half-way. "Maybe it is drugs. Did anyone mess with your medicines?"

Jane shakes her head. "No, I always carry the prescriptions and customs compares the pills to the prescriptions. I even counted them. I thought I might need a refill when I got home. None were missing."

"Then something was hidden in the lining or the backing like Whittington said." Hershey sits next to Jane.

"The bag went through the x-ray machine." Jane tries to remember. "Wouldn't contraband show up on the x-ray?"

Hershey crosses her arms. "I don't know. I just feel like there's some danger in all this."

Jane pats Hershey's arm. "Don't worry. We'll figure this out. We can discuss the whole situation with the others. Five heads are better than two." She pauses. "I think this Whittington fellow has the wrong person and the wrong suitcase. I just wonder how he knows about you."

CHAPTER 6

Magdalene flares the wide nostrils of her long pointed nose before speaking. "Jane! Why on earth didn't you check his credentials before you let him in the house? You have put us all in danger. He may be a maniac, a rapist, a who knows what!"

Jane slowly puts her fork down next to her half-eaten plate of food and looks around at the others. Samuel looks from Magdalene to Jane, back and forth, but continues eating. His fork moves to the twice-baked potato and up to his mouth, down and up, never looking at the plate, never missing a mouthful.

Hershey stares at Jane and chews with her mouth open. She clenches a knife in one hand, a fork in the other. Mimi stops eating altogether with the second flare of nostrils. She mumbles a not-so-silent prayer and thanks God for protecting her from the rapist in Magdalene's warning.

Jane exhales a cleansing breath. "I must apologize for not checking his credentials more closely before he entered our home. I'm afraid I still trust most people unless I have cause for not doing so. The badge looked real and the picture was definitely his."

She picks up her fork but stops mid-air. "Even the police say these con-men are very clever. Their identification looks real to an untrained eye, and I assure you I have an untrained eye."

Magdalene snorts and takes a large gulp of coffee. "Just what is in the suitcase that he wants so badly?"

"I don't know." Jane is exasperated at the ordeal of talking to Magdalene. "If I knew that, I wouldn't have brought any of this up for discussion." She tries to eat again.

"What do you mean?" Magdalene blasts across the table. "Do you mean you wouldn't have told us about this strange man who knows where we live, who could break in at any time and kill us in our beds?"

Mimi starts mumble-praying again. Hershey finally swallows the over-chewed mouthful, and Samuel chokes on a green bean he didn't see coming. Mimi pats him on the back until he resumes normal breathing.

Jane slams her fork down. "Now look what you've done! You're frightening the others. He is not going to kill us or harm us. He is looking for something that might be in the suitcase. I brought this up because I thought you or the others might have some ideas about what he wants. If you can just calm down Magdalene, we may be able to solve this dilemma."

Hershey jumps in. "He kept talking about drugs. I think there might be drugs in the suitcase."

"Customs checked for drugs." Jane resumes her normal speech.

"What about zee peels?" Mimi asks.

"All of my 'peels,' I mean pills were inspected, and I double checked the count." Jane ventures a forkful of food.

"Maybe something was hidden in your papers?" Samuel offers.

Jane dabs her mouth with her napkin. "I looked at all the papers before I filed them, and all of us read the magazine." She stops abruptly and looks at Magdalene. "Maybe there was something in the chocolate truffles."

"Ha!" Magdalene jumps in her seat. "I knew you'd bring up the chocolate sooner or later. How petty of you, Jane. Vivienne has sent me candy for years. I do share a piece with everyone, but it really makes you jealous, doesn't it? You know very well there was nothing in the chocolate."

Jane groans. "I wasn't saying anything about the gift. I just wondered if anyone hid something in the candy. Really Magdalene, these accusations are too much."

"Too much! Too much!" Magdalene jumps to her feet and throws her napkin onto her chair. "Why didn't you ask if the smoked fish contained hidden drugs? Why did you have to bring up the candy? You bought the fish. Why not accuse the fish?"

The room falls silent. Jane's face is bright red. Magdalene gives her a last glower and stomps out of the room.

Mimi quietly says, "We ate zee fish. Eet eez all gone."

Jane's normal skin tone returns. "There was nothing in the fish, and probably nothing in the candy." The desire to eat has left her.

"At least we went over what was in the suitcase." Hershey tries to be helpful. "We eliminated some items, and maybe we'll think of something. Like you said, 'five heads are better than one.'"

Jane doesn't comment. She excuses herself from the table. She's no longer sure about the five heads.

******

Hershey knocks on the open office door. "Anything I can help you with? I'm not needed at the Thrift Shop. Sister Farkas is training new volunteers."

"Thank you, but I'm all caught up." Jane smiles at Hershey. "I'm just finishing my last check of the financial report."

Hershey sits next to the desk and glances at some notes on a yellow pad. "Is that the stuff in your suitcase?"

"It is." Jane sighs. "I decided to list all the items separately. I'm trying to see something I may have missed." She hands the pad to

Hershey, who studies it intently.

The rest of the house is empty and without warning, the back door suddenly creaks. Could it be Whittington? Has some danger returned to their house?

Both stare at each other, each set of eyes growing a little larger. Hershey swallows. Jane swallows. They are in a mirrored pantomime. Hershey never breaks eye contact but quietly puts the pad down, ready to investigate.

The thick fog of fear moving over the room is quickly broken with a chirpy, "Bonjour! Eez anyone home?"

Both women sigh in relief. "We're in here Mimi!" Jane yells.

Mimi in her calf length grey skirt and sneakers has her arms full of notebooks and textbooks from her language class. "I am so glad you are here, chère Hershey. I have wonderful news." Her warm greeting is contagious.

"What is it Mimi?" Jane eagerly asks.

Mimi shuffles through some of her papers. "Bonjour, ma amie Jane." She waves a paper. "Eet eez good news. I meet Sister Duane in zee library. She says all our Sisters at zee retreat house are well. She asks how eez Hershey. We talk about Hershey's lost mind, and Duane says, 'Have we searched the obeets?'"

Mimi shrugs her shoulders for effect. "I say 'I don't know these obeets.' So Duane writes eet down." She points to the paper.

"Obits...obituaries," Jane reads aloud. "She wants us to search the obituaries."

"Oui!" Mimi is very excited. "Maybe the obeets will talk about Hershey. Duane has a computer at zee retreat house, and we are free to use eet any Saturday. Eet makes a good search, and she will help us. If there eez no thing in zee obeets, we can hop on zee Internet. That eez what she says, hop on? I don't know what eez hop on, but eez this not good news? Duane eez so intelligent."

"That is a clever idea." Jane catches Mimi's enthusiasm. "Duane is very good with computers, and the Internet sounds like a good place to search. What do you think, Hershey?"

Hershey shows no sign of interest. "What's the point? We don't even have a name to look up, and I'm not dead. It's just another waste of time."

"No. No, chère Hershey," Mimi moves closer. "You are being the negative. You must have faith."

"Mimi is right," Jane adds. "Obits aren't just names. Sometimes they have pictures. Maybe someone on those Internet waves is looking for you. Maybe that song you remembered will give Duane something to search. What was it again?"

Hershey half-heartedly replies, "*Oh My! Call the FBI.* That song sounds like a bunch of crap."

Mimi looks at Jane. "What eez 'crap'?"

Jane stifles a grin. "Hershey will have to explain that word for you Mimi."

Hershey's mood lightens with Jane's grin. "I'll tell you all about 'crap' on our ride to the retreat house."

Mimi claps her hands and does a little jump. "We are going, bon! We wheel make zee search and find who you are. And I wheel learn about zee 'crap'."

"There is one other thing," Jane interrupts the celebrating. "I'd like you to take the financial report to Monsignor Kelly this afternoon. I'm finishing it now."

Mimi's smiling face drops into a sudden frown. "But ma amie Jane, could not someone else deliver zee report?"

Jane is surprised by Mimi's response. "You've delivered it several times. As a matter of fact, the Monsignor asked if you would be delivering it."

"I do not wish to." Mimi tries to explain. "Monsignor Kelly touches too much."

"I think she means he's a touchy/feely guy," Hershey says, trying to help.

"What!" Jane is shocked.

"I am afraid...," Mimi continues. "The Monsignor, he eez orny." Mimi uses just the right amount of emphasis.

"What did you say?" Jane tightens the grip on her pen.

"She said he's horny," Hershey offers.

"Yes. He eez orny," Mimi repeats. "And not orny for the work of the church. He eez orny for me and all women I think."

Jane tries to comprehend what she is hearing. She was told the Monsignor was cured. He voluntarily took secret treatments in Canada, so he wouldn't hurt anyone again. The Bishop explained that the Monsignor's overt sexual problems were a result of his Vietnam War service. He was supposed to be a reformed man. She had no idea he was harassing Mimi. Her righteous indignation kicks in, and she makes a plan.

"I wish you had told me sooner," she says sympathetically. "But I still want you to deliver this. However, you won't be going alone."

Jane looks at Hershey. "I want you to accompany Mimi. I doubt the Monsignor will do anything inappropriate if you are with her."

"This eez a good plan," Mimi agrees.

Hershey musters bravado. "I'll make sure he stays appropriate."

"I wish I was a fly on the Monsignor's wall when you two arrive," Jane whispers to the departing messengers.

CHAPTER 7

Agent Whittington turns his back to the speaker phone and looks out of the wall of windows in front of him. Miles of skyscrapers form a familiar pattern much like the circuit board for an explosive device. "We did a full trace of the suitcase. It was bought at a church bazaar in Weedsport. The original owner died of natural causes and left everything to that church. Nothing there.

He turns and faces the speaker. "We checked the outer covering for soil samples and only found Syracuse and Paris. We did our own x-rays and took DNA of any piece of hair, skin, dust, dander, or fleck of any kind. They all came back human, mostly Sister Jane Dalton and a smoked fish.

"I think they took it out of the suitcase." He leans into the speaker. "I think they have it in that house. And I am going to get it."

＊＊＊＊＊＊

The Monsignor's secretary is of a non-descript age and smells like lilac and mothballs. She directs Mimi and Hershey to the stiff brocade chairs in the Chancery outer office. "The Monsignor is on the phone with the Bishop," she explains in a hushed tone.

Mimi and Hershey fear a long wait, but it's close to dinner time. Priests seem to be punctual about dinner. Monsignor Kelly comes to the outer office himself. He is over six-feet-tall, nearly bald with bloodshot brown eyes and an exceptionally large upper lip. He moves to Mimi first and jovially extends his hand. "Sister Mimi, so nice to see you again."

Mimi stands and respectfully takes his hand. Her navy-blue suit, white blouse, and silver cross lapel pin make her look like a twelve-year-old Catholic school girl. She is on her best, obedient nun behavior.

Hershey wears a similar blue suit and white blouse but has unbuttoned the top buttons revealing a small edge of her bra. Her trusty black boots put the final touches to her outfit, and her spiky tufts of pink turning brown hair swirl all over her head.

Hershey follows Mimi and also stands. She is behind the Monsignor, so he doesn't see her. His gaze is glued on Mimi.

Mimi tries to disengage her hand which takes some time and effort. "Monsignor Kelly." She points to Hershey. "I would like to introduce our new sister, Sister Hershey Ghirardelli."

The Monsignor scans Hershey slowly, starting with her boots, moving up her legs, breasts, and finally face. Hershey thrusts out her hand. He effervescently grasps it and coos, "My, my, your Sisters do recruit the loveliest girls."

He holds Hershey's hand a little too long. Miss Brine, his secretary, coughs for his attention. "Don't forget your dinner appointment at six."

He continues to hold Hershey's hand. "Thank you Stella. The Bishop has moved it up to five." He finally drops Hershey's hand. "We don't have much time. Let's go to my office."

The two women follow him and he holds the office door for them. They feel his stare on their buttocks as they pass through the portal. His office is sparse with a neatly organized desk and three matching bookcases. Next to his desk are a tan leather sofa and two straight-back chairs.

Mimi sits gingerly at the end of the sofa. Hershey slides next to her. The Monsignor seemingly skips across the room and pulls a chair up close to Mimi. His fruity-smelling aftershave permeates everything.

Mimi's French becomes more nasal. She holds out the manila envelope. "Eet eez zee monthly financial report from Sister Jane."

"Jane is so efficient, always was. She was very lovely when she was your age, just like you. But she did like the communion wine, if you know what I mean. I wonder if she remembers, but that was a long time ago." The Monsignor takes the envelope and rests his hand on Mimi's thigh. "You are always so punctual in delivering the report." He gives her leg a squeeze and moves his hand higher.

Mimi clenches her hands together. She looks to Hershey, who leans into the Monsignor's face and says, "Perhaps you should open the envelope and check the report."

He releases his grip on Mimi. "The report is fine." He tosses it onto his desk. "If all the Moderators were as conscientious as Jane, well I wouldn't have a job would I?" He giggles and turns back to Mimi, who looks plaintively at Hershey. The two women get up and walk toward the door.

The Monsignor is quicker. In a flash, he shuffles between them and the door. "Not going so soon are you?" He pretends to pout. "Why Mimi," he steps closer. She can feel his breath on her cheek. "We haven't practiced our English yet. Remember the anatomy lesson I taught you?"

Mimi's face turns ashen. She moves close enough to Hershey so that their arms touch. Hershey desperately searches for a way to the door.

The Monsignor is oblivious to Hershey. "Let's see, how did we play? Oh yes, I remember." He runs his fingers through Mimi's blonde hair and releases it from behind her ears. Her hair falls loosely onto her face.

"This is head," he begins. "Can you say 'head'?"

Mimi obediently replies, "Head."

The Monsignor rubs his hand down her neck. "This is neck."

Mimi is barely audible. "Neck."

The Monsignor moves his hand to her breast and gives it a squeeze. "This is breast. Can you say 'breast'?"

He has crossed way over the "Be obedient to your superiors" line. Hershey just reacts. She tears his hand off Mimi's breast. "I'd like to do these lessons too. Can I, Monsignor?" She has a tight grip on his hand.

He reluctantly looks away from Mimi and lasciviously eyes Hershey's abundant cleavage. "Of course you can, Sister Hershey." His full attention goes to Hershey's breasts. "Why don't we just skip to where I left off," he oozes.

His breath quickens, and he reaches for a handful of bosom. Hershey responds with a forceful right knee and smashes him mercilessly in the crotch. He clutches his groin, and there is absolute agony on his face. He gasps, "Jane never learned to forgive, did she?"

Mimi grabs Hershey, and they dart out the door. Miss Brine looks up from her desk. "I hope he hasn't forgotten his dinner with the Bishop."

Mimi and Hershey just smile and walk quickly to the elevator.

CHAPTER 8

"How was the trip to the Chancery?" Jane asks.

"Fine, just fine," Hershey and Mimi repeat in unison.

Jane knows that's not true. Her suspicions get worse at eight o'clock when Mimi announces. "I wheel excuse myself for bed. Good night. Zee ride to zee Rushford Retreat House is long. I wheel rest up."

"Goodnight." Jane patiently continues her knitting. She thinks of Magdalene who is sulking in her room, still *in communicato* since their argument.

Samuel is on his way to his room too. He studies several hours each night in preparation for his Practitioner exam. Between his nursing and his studying, he has little time for convent interaction.

He's about to head upstairs when he sees Hershey sitting at the kitchen table. He grabs his backpack from the hall closet and pulls out a folded piece of newspaper which he hands Hershey. "I saw this article when I was in the break room today. It might give you more to search on the Internet. The description of the Senator's daughter sounds a little like you."

He gives her an encouraging smile. But the two of them alone in the kitchen feels suddenly awkward. Without thinking Hershey blurts out. "What are you doing here? I mean living here? Why does a guy want to live in a convent?

Samuel stops and sits next to Hershey. "When I was in Iraq, I had to live with a lot of evil, real evil. Evil people who put bomb vests on disabled kids and sent them to blow up marketplaces. Evil was everywhere like when my two buddies and I were walking back to camp, letting our guard down, letting the day's adrenaline flow back down where it belongs. We were laughing at an old joke when the roadside bomb went off. The explosion threw me down an alley. I wasn't even injured, but my two buddies were dead, killed by the flying shrapnel. I thought it might be a message, but I wasn't hurt, so I was sent back the next day to guard the same street. I had to go back where people weren't human anymore, where feelings were your enemies. Love, concern, attachment, they could get you killed. I didn't feel human anymore either. I wasn't a complex creation of God. I was a mirror of the evil I saw.

"When I got home, my feelings were dead; maybe they were lost in the training or in the constant hyper-vigilance. I was in love when I left for Iraq. She got tired of waiting and married my brother. I liked people before I left. I became a nurse so I could help people, but all those feelings were gone. I thought maybe they should stay that way. If they tried to resurface, I drank them back into submission. That was my life until I met Sister Farkas. She was like a guide back to being human. She was so passionate about everything, except maybe war. She felt so strongly about lifting others up, helping everyone. She could find the good in everyone. When I was with her, I could feel pieces of my squashed soul regenerate. It was like waking up, and I was ready to feel more than hate and pain.

I laughed when she said I should join the Sisters and live in a convent. I didn't know that these small groups of Sisters were welcoming Associates, men and women who could study their Rule, pray with them, and carry on their work. It sounded like a religious Army Reserves especially for someone who really wanted to hide for awhile, like me. So I signed up."

He gets up. "I guess I was done with the alcohol, and I thought this place would be better than sleeping in the back of the Thrift Shop with no shower."

He tries to laugh at the joke. "I've really got to hit the books." He ends the conversation and runs up the stairs.

"Thanks," Hershey says to the vanishing Samuel. She unfolds the newspaper and reads the headline. "Senator's Socialite Daughter Goes Missing."

Hershey sits at the table and carefully reads the article. "Mary Claire Clary, gad-about daughter of Senator Edward Clary has disappeared. She was last seen two weeks ago at *Sister Manchu's Tattoo Parlor* in Albany, New York. The owner and resident artist, Heidi Manchu remembers a Goth-looking customer getting a dragon tattoo in her shop. She reported that when she requested proof of age, the customer showed her a license bearing the name, Mary Claire Clary. The senator's daughter has not been seen since that day. Police are concerned that foul play may be involved. Anyone having information about Mary Claire Clary or her whereabouts is asked to call the Senator's hotline."

"Mary Claire" sounds familiar. Hershey tries to remember something, anything. "Maybe I am his missing daughter! Maybe Whittington works for the government, and he has something to do with the Senator. This is a good lead. This is great!" But with her renewed interest comes an emotional roller-coaster ride.

Who am I really? She rubs her aching temples. *What kind of a person was I…am I?* Her questions have no answers, they just text across her brain. *It was nice of Samuel to think of me today. I wonder if he thinks of me a lot. I think about him.* She shakes her head. *I have to stop this for awhile. I think it's time for a movie.*

Jane sits in a dark corner of the living room. Hershey, totally self-absorbed doesn't see her. "Just what did happen at the Chancery?"

Jane makes Hershey jump. "And don't tell me everything was fine."

"Mimi doesn't want me to tell you what happened." Hershey is painfully aware of her allegiance to both women.

"Why? Why can't you tell me?" Jane is very concerned.

Hershey shrugs her shoulders. "Mimi thinks it's disrespectful because he's a Monsignor and all that obedience stuff."

Jane knows now that something did happen. "Mimi has never been disrespectful. I need to know what happened. Is it the Monsignor?"

Hershey must be loyal to Mimi. "The report is fine. At least that's what he said. He didn't even open it, but he said it was fine."

Jane never thought it would be this hard to get information out of Hershey. Hershey again reminds her of herself. There is no choice but to resort to power and politics. "As the Local Moderator of this community...." She pauses for effect. "I order you to tell me what happened."

Hershey is surprised, but not at all intimidated by Jane's forceful manner. "I'm not really a member of this community, remember?"

"Exactly something I'd say," Jane thinks. She tries another tactic. "As my friend, please tell me what happened?"

Pleading works with Hershey. "Okay, I'll tell you, but Mimi will be upset. I think you might get upset too, upset at me."

Jane's inner voice yells, *"Oh no!"* But she remains calm. "Did you do something, Hershey? Is that what happened?"

"I couldn't really help it." Hershey begins. "I kneed Monsignor Kelly in the balls."

Jane is at first speechless. *Oh God!* Her mind flashes on the image just presented. "You do have a good reason for doing that right?" Jane contemplates the last thirty years of her chosen life. They were meaningful but rather uneventful. The last several months however have taken a bizarre turn. Is this a test?"

"He kept grabbing Mimi." Hershey interrupts Jane's thoughts. "I'm going to tell it to you straight. He wouldn't let us leave. He kept touching Mimi and making her say the parts he touched. Then he grabbed her boob, so I told him he could grab mine. When he did, I just kneed him in the family jewels."

Jane is appalled. Her suspicions never included the brazen audacity of this man. He should be defrocked. He should be charged with sexual harassment. He *should* be kneed in the crotch. She looks at Hershey, who has her eyes closed and is massaging her temples again.

Hershey rubs the side of her head. "Jane, I think I remember something about myself. Have you ever heard the song, *'I Flew So High I Got Burned'*?"

Not another song! Jane is still raging with anger at Monsignor Kelly. "I'm not very good with songs." She is immediately sorry for her shortness when she sees the concern, mixed with sadness, that creeps into Hershey's face.

Jane softens her voice. "Maybe music is a clue to who you are. Maybe you can look up these songs and find some information that will help you."

Hershey gives a weak smile. "They're pretty weird songs though, aren't they?"

"Maybe not weird," Jane offers. "Just modern. You must like modern music. And thank you for telling me about the Monsignor. You are a good friend."

Jane starts to leave. "I need to talk to Magdalene. She's really in charge of Mimi's formation while she's living with us. Magdalene may want to discuss this with you too."

Hershey shrugs again. Right now, she's more interested in watching the movie.

******

Jane goes to Magdalene's room. She must tell her about the Monsignor Kelly incident and hopes to omit the "kneed in the crotch" part. She steadies herself outside Magdalene's door and taps lightly.

Magdalene opens the door a few inches and pokes out her beak-like nose. "Yes?" She says in her controlled whisper.

"I need to speak to you." Jane gains some confidence.

"Concerning?" Magdalene asks in the same tone.

Jane doesn't show her annoyance. "Concerning an incident between Sister Mimi and Monsignor Kelly."

Magdalene opens the door more and gives Jane a blank look.

"You are Novice Mistress or whatever we're calling it now." Jane says impatiently. "You are in charge of formation for Sister Mimi and Brother Samuel. You need to know what Mimi has been enduring every time she delivers the financial report to the Chancery."

Magdalene's facial expression turns to deep interest. She opens the door. "Come in."

Jane sits on the chair next to the small corner desk. "I'm sorry to intrude on your privacy like this Maggie, but I'm very upset. I know you will be too."

"You haven't called me Maggie in years." Magdalene concentrates on twisting her wristwatch back into place. "Before we talk about Mimi, we need to forgive each other."

Oh no! Not the forgiveness! Jane screams inside her head. "Of course." She bows her head. "Please forgive me, Maggie. I know I'm not always as sensitive to your feelings as I should be. I know I'm often selfish about what I think is right."

Jane has a sudden revelation, a thought that comes out of nowhere. She accepts it as an intuitive message that will direct her future. "Maggie, I promise I will resign my position as Moderator right after the Chapter meeting in Iowa.

"You're forgiven, Jane." Magdalene's tone returns to normal. "I'm glad you're resigning. I think all of the responsibility and paper work is bad for you. I don't want you drinking again."

Her voice is softer now and seemingly sincere. She's the other Maggie, the sensitive friend that Jane often has to hunt for because she hides behind her bluster. "I never want to see you in one of those asylums again. I couldn't bear to see you like that again."

Jane tries to respond, tries to put Maggie's fears to rest. "That was over forty years ago. I haven't had a drink in forty years. They don't even have places like that anymore."

"It was horrible." Magdalene's voice cracks. "They did horrible things to you in there. I tried to come every week, but we couldn't travel alone. No one else would come. Sometimes you didn't even recognize me. The doctor told Mother Superior to stop my visits. He said it was bad for you to see me. I told her he was wrong, but she believed him. And...I...I...left you there all alone until you were finally released." Magdalene's eyes well up with tears.

Jane feels deep compassion for Magdalene. This is the other side of Maggie, the side that isn't afraid, that recognizes love and friendship as normal parts of our being. But Jane doesn't want to deal with these memories right now. There are more immediate problems to attend to. She doesn't have the strength to be in the present and the past at the same time, so she pushes these memories back into a dark corner of her mind.

"You are also forgiven, Maggie." Jane reaches over and touches Magdalene's face. "Although, there is nothing to forgive. I knew you couldn't come. They made a point of telling me I was all alone. They were mean that way. They didn't realize that I took as true what you said on your last visit. You told me, 'I will pray for you always, because I love you.' I held onto those words. I knew you were praying, and I joined my prayers with yours. And see, I'm fine. I'm even a big deal with the same community that left me all alone." Jane smiles.

Magdalene accepts this cue that Jane doesn't want to talk about her past anymore. She takes a small handkerchief from her sweater pocket and lightly blows her nose. "Now, what happened to Mimi at the Chancery that is bad enough for you to remember I'm in charge of her formation?"

Jane appreciates Magdalene's return to grumpiness. "Remember how we all agreed that it would be good for Mimi to deliver the monthly report and get all that experience using her English?"

Magdalene nods and listens attentively. "It seems the rumors about Monsignor Kelly and his flirtatious ways are true, but his ways are much more than flirtatious. He has sexually harassed Mimi each time she's gone there. Mimi thought it would be disrespectful if she told us."

Jane shakes her fist. "I am so angry at that over-sexed, old lecher that I could punch him in the nose."

Magdalene responds quickly. "Jane, that is Monsignor Kelly you're talking about."

"He shouldn't be a Monsignor. He shouldn't be a priest! He's the same bastard he was twenty-years-ago," Jane practically yells. "I can't believe we sent that poor unknowing girl over there alone. I can't believe that he actually molested her."

Magdalene wrinkles her forehead. "All right, try to calm down and tell me exactly what happened. Tell me exactly as Mimi told you."

"Mimi didn't tell me," Jane explains. "I had to order the truth out of Hershey. Mimi swore her to silence, but I knew something was wrong. It was the way they behaved when they got home."

"If this story is coming only from Hershey," Magdalene begins. "Well, I must admit that I am very skeptical about anything she says. She isn't like the rest of us. She appears a little maladjusted."

Magdalene chooses her words carefully. "Her behavior may be

the result of the swelling in her head or the amnesia, but it is strange. I'm not sure we should take her word about this."

Jane controls her response. "I agree with you, Maggie."

Magdalene is genuinely surprised. She expected Jane to protest the negative comments about Hershey.

"I agree," Jane repeats. "I was also skeptical until Hershey told me how she tried to help Mimi. She may have...," Jane hunts for the words. "May have hurt the Monsignor while helping Mimi."

"I told you that woman was dangerous!" Magdalene responds.

Jane cuts her off. "The Monsignor did not call us to report the incident. Don't you find that strange?"

Jane doesn't wait for Magdalene to reply. "He groped Mimi's leg and her breast. I'm quite sure this isn't the first time. Both Hershey and Mimi are going to the Retreat House tomorrow, but I think you should talk to Mimi before she leaves. If you believe her story, we will need to decide what to do."

Jane stands to leave. Magdalene stands too. "I'll speak with Mimi. Don't worry Jane, I will find out the truth. You know I don't want anyone taking advantage of these young girls."

Jane remembers Maggie forty years earlier, trying to right every wrong and often putting herself in danger to protect others. Jane spontaneously gives Maggie a big hug. Magdalene is taken off guard and can only half-hug back.

Jane understands. "Good night, Maggie."

CHAPTER 9

Before Hershey and Mimi leave for Rushford, Magdalene insists on a private meeting with Mimi. Hershey waits in the kitchen, nervously drumming her fingers on the table and playing with the car keys. After forty minutes, Mimi finally emerges from Magdalene's room. Her eyes are red and swollen. "We wheel go now, Hershey," she says quietly.

They get into the worn 1995 Escort and ride in silence for the first fifteen minutes. Hershey thinks Mimi is angry. *Maybe she feels betrayed because I told Jane about the Monsignor.* Hershey opens her mouth to say something then closes it and just sighs. The awkward silence continues as they ride past various cities and small towns. Mimi is ten miles over the speed limit when four sparrows unexpectedly swoop in front of the car. They are followed by a silver circular object with short steel wings.

The shiny silver ball stops abruptly and flies back in front of the windshield. Mimi swerves to avoid hitting it. "Mère Marie!"

"Watch out!" Hershey yells. Her body jerks sideways, and she bumps her head on the passenger window.

Mimi reaches for Hershey's arm. "Are you okay, chère?"

"I'm fine." Hershey rubs her head. "But what was that?"

"Eet is only zee Mobeel Flying Unit. Eet takes pictures." She thinks for a moment. "And eet must chase zee little birds."

"I don't think I've ever heard of any of those." Hershey is relieved that Mimi is talking. "What do they take pictures of?"

Mimi's attention is back on her driving. "Eet takes pictures of people mostly, maybe some buildings. Eet belongs to the IIA, the International Intelligence Agency. We have seen many of the Mobeel Flying Units in France especially around our convent.

"I can't remember anything about a flying unit." Hershey gingerly touches the bump on her head. "I thought a second bump on the head brings back your memory. I still don't know who I am."

This makes Mimi smile. "Do not worry. I have prayed to St. Theresa to help us recover you today. She never fails."

"I'm...I'm really sorry," Hershey bravely ventures an apology. "Jane ordered me to tell her what happened. She knew something was wrong."

Hershey waits for Mimi to respond. "Not that I take orders very well, but I was really mad at that guy. He had no right to treat you like that. I thought maybe Jane could get him fired or something."

"Priests do not get fired, chère." Mimi's voice returns to its normal buoyancy. "A bad priest eez hard to correct." She pauses. "I am not mad at you. I was feeling, how do you say, shamed about zee actions with him. I am better now. Magdalene believed me." Mimi gives Hershey a quick glance. "She eez sorry eet happened. Eet wheel not happen again. I no longer have to go to zee Chancery."

There is another pause before she adds, "Magdalene also asks what you deed to zee Monsignor. I was not sure what to say."

Hershey sheepishly asks, "What did you tell her?"

"I say you poosh him away. And Magdalene say, 'Do not worry. Enjoy your day at the Retreat House.' and now all is *bon*...good."

Hershey isn't sure all is *bon*, but she moves on. "I have a new lead on my identity." She takes the newspaper article out of her grey jacket pocket. "Samuel gave me this article. It's about this missing woman, a senator's daughter who got a tattoo at a *Sister Manchu's Tattoo Parlor.*

"Oh zee Sister Manchu!" Mimi responds.

"Yeah, the Chinese Sister." Hershey continues. "The other thing is this girl's name is Mary Claire which sounds really familiar to me, and she has a dragon tattoo."

"Marie Claire? Eet is French. Perhaps you are French?" Mimi offers.

Hershey shrugs. "It's a good lead anyway. Think we can check it out on the computer?"

"I am sure…" Mimi is a little hesitant. "I am not so familiar with the searches, but Sister Duane eez not only good with her university work but an expert with zee computer. She wheel help us. She knows how we can find you."

Mimi smiles at the road ahead and starts whistling a French folksong.

Hershey catches Mimi's confidence for a brief moment but a sudden knot in her stomach reminds her of the fear that often comes with knowledge.

******

The Rushford Retreat House is an old mansion donated to the Syracuse Diocese. It was once used as a summer getaway for the Bishop and his fellow priests. It became less and less popular because it was isolated and didn't have a golf course. After being empty and unused for several years, it was loaned to the Sisters of St. Francis Dupre.

Sister Duane and the five other Sisters who live there brought new life to the house. They opened it up to retreats for all the religious communities in the region. It also provides space for secular retreats and business meetings.

Mimi drives slowly down the long winding driveway. The majesty of the house and its wooded setting are breathtaking. The three story mansion is white stucco with red brick outlines around the windows and doors. Four marble columns hold up the large entrance canopy where an ornately carved double door opens out to matching brick steps and the brick driveway.

******

Hershey and Mimi are escorted by Sister Duane through the large country kitchen to the library. Two entire walls are lined with books. The third holds a large fireplace made of rough stone and green tiles. The far wall is made up of floor to ceiling windows that look out onto rolling hills and flower gardens.

The computer is close to the windows. Duane clicks the mouse and opens to the Internet. Like a dedicated teacher, she has written down several Internet addresses that might be helpful in searching a name. Mimi interrupts the lesson to show Duane the newspaper article. "How can we find eef zee Marie Claire Clary is our Hershey?" she asks.

"It's Mary Claire Clary," Hershey corrects the first name.

"That's an easy one," Duane explains. "Just do a search for her name. Type it on this search line and hit enter."

A complete page of listings for Mary Claire Clary comes up on the screen with options for several more pages. "It may take some time to go through all of this," Duane explains. "And you still have other subjects to search."

She gives a thumbs up and turns to leave. "I have to attend the South American Mission Meeting, but I'll be back to take you to lunch." She gives them an encouraging wave.

Hershey squints at the screen. "I don't know anything about computers, I don't think."

"I am okay." Mimi studies the search engine list. "I use zee college library computer. I search for magazine articles. Eet eez zee same, maybe." She leans closer. "Look at all of zee informations about Marie Claire."

"It's Mary Claire." Hershey tries again. "The article said she was popular with the social set, and I may not have mentioned it." Hershey lowers her voice. "But she was arrested several times for driving while impaired."

"What is this 'Driving while in pairs'?" Mimi asks.

"Not pairs," Hershey explains. "*Impaired.* It means driving when you are drunk or on drugs."

"Oh, she eez a wild one," Mimi comments nonchalantly and clicks on the first entry.

"That's the article that Samuel gave me," Hershey says excitedly. "But it didn't have a picture with it. That looks like a license photo or a mug shot."

Mimi studies the picture. "Zee photo ees not so clear. She has zee hair covering her eyes and nose."

"She does seem to be hiding behind her long bangs," Hershey agrees. "Do you think she looks like me?"

"I do not think she looks like anyone." Mimi clicks the second entry.

A short article appears telling of the arrest of Mary Claire Clary for driving her sports car through a pita bread bakery. The article reads: "Ms. Clary's alcohol level was over the allowed limit. She was lucky that no one was hurt. Fortunately at three o'clock in the morning, the bakery was closed."

The next article is also about an arrest. "Mary Claire Clary was stopped for speeding last Thursday. She claimed to be on her way home from a birthday party. Witnesses claim she was not invited to the party. Her alcohol level was over the allowed limit."

"I'm not sure I want to know any more." Hershey moans. "I don't think I want to be Mary Claire Clary."

"We are who we are, chère," Mimi offers. "We can always change." She clicks the next site and four photos from a paper called *Insider Dirt* appear on the screen.

The first photo is a Corvette that has smashed into a telephone pole. The caption reads, "Mary Claire Clary is Drunk and Does It Again."

The second picture is of six young women all dressed in black leather slacks, skirts, jackets and boots being herded into police cars. The caption reads, "Children of the rich and famous arrested at a drug party."

"The faces are too small to really see," Hershey comments.

Mimi takes off her glasses and leans forward. "Yes, they are too small and all zee boots have zee high heels. You do not come with zee high heels."

She clicks the third picture. It is a distinguished-looking, grey-haired gentleman hugging a long-haired, younger woman whose back is to the camera. The caption reads, "Senator Clary welcomes his daughter home after her court-imposed stay in rehab."

"Her back is to the camera." Hershey gets closer to the screen.

Mimi studies the picture and points to the woman's shoulder. "Do you see where zee blouze eez off her shoulder?"

Hershey takes a long look. "Oh wow! She's wearing that off the shoulder, so everyone can see her tattoo."

"Ma oui." Mimi slips into her French. "Zee tattoo, does eet not look familiar?"

"It's my dragon. She has the dragon on her shoulder." Hershey looks at Mimi. "You know what this means? I'm not Mary Claire Clary. I don't have the tattoo on my shoulder. I don't have any tattoo on my shoulder. It's on my…well, you know where it is."

"Oh yes, chèrie." Mimi nods in agreement. "I am sorry you are not zee Marie Claire. But eef you only have the one dragon and eet is where you sit, then it cannot be on your shoulder, and you are not zee wild girl."

Hershey isn't sure if she should feel disappointed or relieved. "Let's at least look at the last picture," she says half-heartedly.

This photo is a close-up of Mary Claire Clary. She is holding up the front of her shirt revealing another tattoo. This one is the head of a Tiki God whose mouth is her bellybutton.

The caption reads, "Mary Claire has another one, and she got it at her favorite tattoo parlor." Mary Claire's face is very clear in this picture, and she is not Hershey.

"Do you have zee big head on your stomach?" Mimi asks.

"No," Hershey promptly answers. "That's definitely not me." She looks at the picture again. "But look at the letters on the window behind her. Doesn't it say, "Manchu?""

Mimi looks. "Eet could be. Perhaps we steel have zee clue."

"We know there's a tattoo parlor in Albany." Hershey writes in her notebook. "And she did have a tattoo like mine. Maybe we can check out the tattoo?" Hershey gets very animated. "Maybe we belong to the same club or organization? Or maybe we hang around together. I think this tattoo place might have some answers."

"Eet ees a good idea." Mimi catches the enthusiasm. "Maybe though for now, we should change to the other searches. I think we should try zee name search." She types in www.obits.com. The screen asks for "city" and "state." "We are not sure eef this eez your city, but you are here." Mimi types in "Syracuse, New York."

A long list of names appears on the screen. Mimi quickly scrolls down searching for "Ghirardelli". The closest is "Ghiratolli." She clicks the name and an antique photo of a ninety-year-old woman appears. A detailed obituary is next to the photo.

"That's not me." Hershey is already discouraged. "That may not even be my real name."

"Do not get zee frustrations," Mimi says. "We must begin somewhere."

She returns to the obituaries and searches, "Hershey." There are twelve. Most have pictures; none are this Hershey. The ones without pictures have ages or illnesses. All easily eliminate Sister Hershey.

Hershey looks at Mimi. "What next?"

Mimi types in "www.deaths.com" and "New York."

They both scan the long list for "Ghirardelli"or "Hershey." Nothing is there. They continue with Duane's suggestions. These include missing persons, kidnapped persons, persons wanted by the police, and "Itinerant Wives." Just as they finish the last itinerant wife, Duane returns to escort them to lunch.

The retreat center's formal dining room is as large as St. Mary's Cathedral. Three multi-tiered chandeliers hang from a gold-leafed curved ceiling. Three long mahogany tables are lined up under the chandeliers with matching mahogany chairs on either side of the tables.

The Diocesan Evangelical Renewal group is at the first table eagerly awaiting the food. Several Vietnamese Sisters in blue habits sit at the second table and nod as Duane passes by. The last table is occupied by three of the elderly Sisters of St. Francis Dupre. They have chosen to spend their waning years at the Retreat House making rosaries for their South American missions.

Mimi, Hershey, and Duane join this friendly group. Mimi gives a brief update of the lives of the Syracuse sisters including Sister Farkas who chose not to live at the Retreat House.

"She felt a calling to minister to the poor," explains Sister Elsberth. "She's very familiar with the Thrift Store neighborhood, you know. She was born right in that tavern, O'Hoolihans. Her mother was a barmaid there."

This revelation brings on a new discussion of hometowns, declining neighborhoods, and the need for outreach. All agree that

Sister Farkas, unlike the others, still has the physical energy for outreach.

"Each must serve in her own way," observes Sister Melborn. "There comes a time when you know your limitations, so you find another way to serve like making rosaries."

This leads to the presentation of handmade rosaries to Mimi and Hershey. There are several "Thank yous and God bless yous," and Duane leads the before meal prayer.

Hershey pokes at her roast beef and lines up her string beans in a fence-like pattern. Duane asks how the search is going. "Hershey eez not Marie Claire," Mimi answers. "But she may be her friend. We deed zee obeets and have no more lists."

Duane turns to the sullen Hershey. "Don't be discouraged. These searches take time."

Hershey doesn't look up. "What search? I think we're finished."

"You've just started." Duane gives a little laugh "You haven't gone to any of the social networking sites or the blogs. There's a blog for every topic in the world including missing persons. You also need to think of anything you can remember, back from when you woke up in the hospital. Think about anything that can be a key word for a search. Maybe a birthmark, an allergy, a food you like. I'm sure there's a cabbage lover's blog out there."

Mimi is energized by this new challenge. "You see chère Hershey. We've just started. St. Theresa eez still working."

"There is the tattoo," Hershey offers halfheartedly.

"Yes, zee dragon!" Mimi adds.

"You have a tattoo?" Duane is surprised and a little curious.

Hershey gets more enthusiastic. "Maybe we can search for those song titles that keep running through my head."

Duane reluctantly leaves the subject of the tattoo and explains how to access song titles. "You can put in the title and find the writer, performer, and even related information."

"For the tattoo…" She tries to get back to an interesting topic. "Just type 'dragon tattoo' or 'Sister Manchu's Tattoo parlor' on the search line. Try to narrow it down and follow the links. Where is your tattoo, Hershey?" she asks inquisitively.

Hershey doesn't hear her. She feels like eating now. All of her concentration is focused on finishing her food before it is cleared.

Duane postpones her curiosity, and everyone in the dining hall "ahhhs" as the miniature flaming cakes are placed before them. Dessert becomes the final lunch topic of conversation.

Mimi and Hershey spend an hour on the tattoo search. They view seventy-three images of dragon tattoos, none match Hershey's. They search "Sister Manchu's Tattoo Parlor" and find an address and phone number and twenty sample tattoos. One is Hershey's dragon. When they return to Syracuse, she'll call the number and see if anyone remembers her.

"Let's try one more search," Hershey suggests. "Then we need to get home."

Mimi agrees. "What shall I type in?"

Hershey thinks for a minute. "Let's look up the songs."

"What eez zee song name?"

"Let's try, '*I Flew So High I Got Burned*'," Hershey answers.

Mimi stops typing and bows her head. "I ask St. Theresa to get with eet." She clicks the first entry and it opens to a page of sheet music. The top of the page reads, "*I Flew So High I Got Burned*" by Harley David, recorded by *Talking Trash*."

"Do you recognize any of zee names?" Mimi asks.

Hershey   reads   slowly   and   deliberately, "T…a…l…k…i…n…g…Trash?"

Mimi clicks the name and two color posters appear. Mimi double-clicks the left poster. It fills the page. Two androgynous beings wearing black lipstick and exaggerated eye-makeup are spitting fireworks, maybe sparklers, from their mouths. Both have short, spiky hot pink and green hair similar to Hershey's earlier appearance. Both singers wear black leather vests with fringe, black leather pants with the cheeks cut out and black leather boots that look just like Hershey's. Their face each other, so it's difficult to see their features.

Mimi asks, "Do you recognize anyone?"

Hershey's eyes are glued to the poster. "No."

Mimi double-clicks the other poster. This one is of the same two singers, in the same makeup with the same clothing but is a closer head shot. Both face the camera with their tongues grotesquely touching their chins. Under each head shot is a name. The singer on the right is "Wolfgang Merge." On the left is "Sky Volta," who, eerily, resembles Hershey.

"I don't recognize any of the names," Hershey says quickly. "But don't you think the one on the left looks a little like me?"

Mimi clicks the "Print" button. She scans the top of the page and finds "Band Background and Information." She clicks on that and both read the paragraphs that appear.

"Talking Trash was formed in 2000 and stormed to the top of the charts selling 600,000 copies of their first album, *"Stink."* They toured America, England, Australia, and Japan non-stop for two years. In 2004, lead singers Sky Volta A.K.A. Mary Margaret O'Brien and Wolfgang Merge A.K.A. Dave Hill pooled their earnings and formed their own label: *Sudden-Death Records.*

Since then, *Sudden-Death* has recorded such Alternative rock groups as Flaming Coyote, Barren Seed, and Eat This. *Sudden-Death* was sold to *MadNight Records* in 2008, the same year Sky Volta and Wolfgang Merge got married in a Gothic ceremony in Dublin, Ireland.

Both performers are now retired and unavailable to fans. They occasionally make guest appearances at charity benefits."

Mimi clicks "Print" again. "Zee singers have many names, no?"

"Mary Margaret O'Brien sounds familiar." Hershey unconsciously rubs her temples again. "I know I said that about Mary Claire Clary, but I think Mary Margaret O'Brian really might be my name."

"So." Mimi tries to be reassuring. "You are maybe Irish not Italian?"

"I can't be sure." Hershey is visibly upset. "I can't believe I'm one of those...those... *Trash Talkers*. That name sounds a little familiar too. But I can't remember any weird stuff like alternative rock, Gothic wedding, and Japan."

"There eez punk rocks in France," Mimi offers. "Eet eez just show business."

Hershey walks to the printer and gets the papers. "At least I have more clues." She looks at the pictures again. "I can track down the recording company and maybe talk to someone who knows these singers."

Mimi shuts down the computer. "Eet eez already dark. We need to start home."

Hershey just sighs as they walk out into the clear evening. Mimi starts the engine and guides the old car back down the long driveway. Soon they are on the Thruway heading home.

CHAPTER 10

It's after ten o'clock when Mimi and Hershey pull into the convent driveway. The house is dark except for the bright backdoor light. This means that even Jane went to bed early. Mimi turns the car lights off before entering the driveway, so as not to wake her sleeping Sisters and Brother.

Hershey studies the parked car across the street.

"What eez wrong?" Mimi asks.

"Probably nothing." Hershey gets out of the car and quietly closes her door.

Mimi also gets out and noiselessly closes her door. Hershey keeps watching the parked car, so Mimi walks over to Hershey and also stares at the car.

"I think that's the same car that Whittington guy drove. It's hard to see if anyone is inside with those shaded windows." She finally looks at Mimi. "Oh, let's go in. I'm imagining things. I probably need food and some sleep."

Mimi gives Hershey a reassuring smile and leads the way to the door. She searches in her purse for the house keys and looks up at Hershey once more. The overhead light falls on Mimi like a spotlight, and Hershey suddenly sees it!

She can't believe her eyes! There's an obvious aura around Mimi's head. The light breaks into glowing particles that circle Mimi's head.

It's the aura of a saint…no… no…of an angel. Mimi looks radiant in her dull grey suit. The aura around her head is glowing and shimmering. *Mimi is glowing like a heavenly angel.*

Mimi catches Hershey staring at her. "Is anything wrong chère?"

Hershey is speechless. Her eyes are focused on the aura. She searches for a proper prayer.

"Chère Hershey…" Mimi tries to get a response. "Is something on my head?" She reaches up and carefully touches above her head. She feels them and starts making frightened squeaky noises. She waves her hand and jumps up and down. "Get them away! Get them away!"

Confused but still aware of alarm when she sees it, Hershey runs over and helps Mimi wave away the aura. It finally seems to form a straight line and moves away from the light.

"What was that?" Hershey asks.

Mimi composes herself. "They are zee sand flies. They are always near the light. Hurry, do not let them in." She unlocks the door and scoots in. Hershey follows.

They reach the kitchen, and Mimi continues to brush off the now invisible sand flies. She turns to Hershey and whispers, "Good night, chère, I am more tired than hungry. Please do not worry. We wheel unwrinkle who you are tomorrow. Jane wheel help us."

She moves to the stairs. Her pleasant confidence pushes away some of Hershey's instinctive concern. *Maybe she really is an angel, or maybe St. Theresa is at work?* Hershey feels a little crazy. Maybe it's the excitement of finding out all that information, the band, the tattoo.

She decides to leave Jane a note. If she reads it before morning prayers, she could put some time aside for them to meet. Hershey walks toward the office. The door is open, unusual for this time of evening.

Her heart begins to beat a little louder, a little faster. Something's wrong. She feels it in her stomach, in her chest. Her brain sends out loud signals. "Danger! Danger!" She pushes against the door, and it opens a few more inches. She sees Jane's desk. Papers are everywhere, scattered across the top, on the chair, all over the floor. The file draws are also open. Folders and papers are overflowing the drawers.

She gives the door a push and cautiously enters the room. No one is visible. She takes a few more steps into the room, and something moves behind her. She whirls around and sees a tall figure in a dark ski mask. The sinister figure gives her a fierce shove, and she falls backwards into the desk chair. She takes the chair down to the floor with her.

"Damn it! Hey you! Stop! Stop! Help! Someone help!" Hershey tries to get up.

Her screams send the intruder running into the living room. They also bring Jane and Magdalene running from their bedrooms. Magdalene, struggling into a long robe and Jane in her flannel nightgown reach the office at the same time. Magdalene looks at the papers and disarray in the office and freezes. Jane runs immediately to the fallen Hershey.

Hershey yells, "He's getting away!" while Jane tries to disentangle her from the chair. "Get him! He's in the living room!" Hershey screams at Magdalene.

Magdalene does not move. Hershey is safely on her feet, and Jane rummages through the papers to find the phone. Hershey pushes past Magdalene and runs into the living room. A chair has been pulled into the entranceway, so she has to push it out of the way.

She makes it to the living room, but it's too late. One of the front windows is wide open. Hershey sees the taillights of the now familiar car as it turns a corner and disappears.

Jane hurries behind Hershey. She has a heavy cross paperweight in her upraised hand.

"He got away." Hershey tries to slow down her breathing. Both women stare out the open window. Jane finally lowers the brass cross and puts it on a nearby table. She closes and locks the window. Magdalene enters and frantically announces, "I've called the police! They should be here any minute!"

She looks from Hershey to Jane. "We've been burglarized! Dear Lord! What next?"

Jane ignores the remark and asks, "Are you hurt, Hershey?"

Hershey shakes her head. "No."

Jane is about to ask again when Mimi and Samuel come running into the living room. Samuel takes the lead. "What's going on?"

"We've been burglarized," Magdalene repeats.

"Robbed?" Samuel asks.

"Robins? What? Are zee robins in zee house?" Mimi asks.

"A thief," Samuel explains, moving into defense mode.

Mimi presses her hands to her mouth and promptly pulls them away. "Thiefs in zee house! Oh no!"

Before Samuel can correct any more grammar or move into the living room, two wailing, lights-flashing police cars race up to the house. Four officers run up the driveway with their hands on their guns. Two go to the side entrance, and two keep running to the back of the house.

Jane heads for the kitchen door with Hershey right behind her. The other ducks in a row follow. The first officer enters, police baton in hand. "I'm Officer Kusnicki. Is he still here?"

"No. He jumped out the front window and drove away," Jane answers calmly.

The second officer enters, "Officer Roland. Anybody hurt?" He pauses. "Does anybody need an ambulance?"

"Everyone's okay," Hershey answers.

"He did assault her." Magdalene nervously points to Hershey.

She has retrieved Jane's robe and is helping her put it on.

Officer Roland steps closer to Hershey. "Are you hurt? Do you need medical help?"

A picture of her last trip to the hospital flashes into Hershey's head. "I'm fine. He just pushed me. I fell over. I'm fine. I don't need any help."

Officer Roland joins his partner in the living room. Officer Kusniki has the window open again. They both examine the frame. Kusniki yells out the window to one of the officers. "Check around here for footprints or anything you can find."

He brings his head back in and turns to Jane, who appears to be the spokeswoman. "It wasn't hard for him to break in. Those old screens just pop off. Someone left this window unlocked. He didn't even have to force it open, just pushed it up. So what did he steal, Sister?" He looks at Samuel. "You are all religious, right? Whoever called 911 said this is a convent."

"Yes, we are Sisters and this is Brother Samuel." Magdalene carefully pronounces every word. She senses that Officer Kusniki is being condescending. "These windows are never left unlocked. They are never opened."

"When was the last time you checked 'em?" Kusniki asks.

"We don't need to check them." Magdalene is steadfast. "We never open them."

Jane tries to deescalate this discussion. "Perhaps when that phony FBI agent, the scam-artist was here a few days ago, he unlocked the window. We were in the basement for quite some time getting the suitcase for him."

Neither officer knows what Jane is talking about. She briefly details her police report concerning Whittington and the idea that he was an imposter. "He seems to be looking for something specific," Jane adds. "He doesn't seem to be satisfied with the suitcase. What could he possibly want?"

"Maybe he cased your place when he was here," Officer Kusniki offers. "Maybe he just pretended he wanted the suitcase. He might be looking for money, or charge cards, or identity stuff in your papers. Identity theft is big business right now."

"Sisters and our Associates don't use a lot of charge cards, and we don't have much money," Jane says.

Undaunted, the officer continues, "We'll try and catch this guy and find out what he was after."

He takes a description of the intruder, as much as Hershey can remember. He also takes a description of Whittington. He looks up from his notebook. "If you find anything missing give us a call, and we'll add it to the report."

Officer Roland jumps in. "What about the car? How about a description of that?"

Hershey does her best. "It was a late-model, dark-green Lincoln, I think, a four door with a large antenna on the back trunk."

"What about the license number?" Kusniki continues writing.

Hershey tries to rub some recall into her mind, but the stress and excitement are taking their toll. "I didn't get the license number."

"Too bad." Kusniki finally looks up.

"I know zee number," Mimi chirps.

"You do?" Hershey and Kusniki say in unison.

"Yes, Eet reminds me of my sister, Elise."

Everyone falls into puzzled silence. Officer Kusniki asks, "What is the license number?"

"Eet is E like Elise and A like Andrea, her confirmation name." Mimi speaks slowly and deliberately. "1 like January. A 71, zee year she eez born. And 03, her baby's age."

The officer reads it back, "EA17103?" Mimi nods affirmatively.

"That's amazing." He turns to Jane. "We'll run this through the computer. Everything looks secure now, so you should all feel safe. Try to get some sleep."

Kusniki and Roland join the officers outside, and the last police car finally pulls away. Jane suggests they all have some chamomile tea. The dazed little group sips in silence.

Samuel finds it hard to stay awake and since the "all clear" has been sounded, he goes back to bed. Mimi follows, but not until she rinses the cups and saucers. Magdalene gets up and grumbles all the way back to her room. Jane tries to leave, but Hershey insists they double-check all the locks and the windows.

Everyone is finally in bed, but Samuel is the only one asleep. Mimi says her rosary. Hershey studies the press release for *Talking Trash*. Jane makes another list of what was in the suitcase. And Magdalene tosses and turns, mumbling just loud enough for Jane to overhear, "Raped and killed in our beds!"

CHAPTER 11

Jane, Magdalene, Mimi and Hershey spend the next morning cleaning and organizing the tossed office. Jane returns disorganized papers to their rightful folders while Hershey works on the overturned desk drawers. Magdalene places the office supplies in their proper place on top of the desk.

No one speaks except Mimi, who thanks the Virgin Mother for once again sparing Hershey's life. "Merci, Mère Marie."

Hershey solemnly repeats, "Thank you, Mary."

When the phone rings, everyone jumps. Jane answers it. "Yes, Officer Kusniki." She faces the others trying to include them in the conversation. "Yes, I remember you from last night. This is Sister Jane Dalton. Yes, the one in charge. Yes, the one who lost the suitcase."

Jane falls silent. Her expression turns from hopeful interest to puzzlement. A few moments pass before she breaks her silence. "Are you saying you know who broke into the house, but you can't tell me? Yes, I understand. You traced the license number, and it's a government car. What branch of the government?" She waits again. "The FBI?"

She listens intently, as do all the others in the room. "Not the FBI, but the International Intelligence Agency, the IIA. No, I'm not familiar with them. Really, all over the world, matters of national security and safety. Why didn't he just tell me the truth? Why didn't he say who he worked for and what he wanted?" Jane rolls her eyes. The others look at each other, but no one speaks.

"Yes. Yes. You have my word." Jane shifts to her reassuring voice. "I do realize you're a good Catholic, and you went to Catholic school. The Sisters were kind. No. I will not put your job in jeopardy. I appreciate your help, and I will take your advice. Thank you, Officer Kusniki, Stanley Joseph. God bless you and goodbye."

Jane hangs up and faces the three anxious onlookers. "That was Officer Stanley Joseph Kusniki, one of the few people who enjoyed his Catholic School experience. Out of allegiance to his first grade teacher, Sister Immaculata Fortunata, he's put his job at risk to tell me things he shouldn't." Jane takes a breath.

"He was supposed to tell me that they couldn't trace the license plate number," Jane continues. "Stanley Joseph was to assure me that a robber working this neighborhood, our probable intruder, was caught last night. Instead, he told me the car belongs to the International Intelligence Agency. He doesn't know why they broke in. But if I have something they want, I should give it to them because they won't go away. No one can stop the IIA. They are protectors of our national security." She finally sits.

"Just what does all that mean?" Magdalene sits too.

Hershey doesn't wait for Jane, but answers Magdalene. "That means Whittington, or whatever his name is, can come creeping in here anytime he wants to until he finds whatever he's looking for."

"Is that true, Jane?" Magdalene turns from Hershey to Jane.

"I'm afraid so." Jane is pensive and quiet. "The police can't stop him. I just wish I knew what he wanted. I'd give it to him."

Magdalene stands in righteous indignation. "Jane, call him up and tell him we don't have it! Tell him to stop breaking into our house!"

Mimi interrupts. "Eet eez not so easy, ma Magdalene. Zee CIA,

INTERPOL, and IIA are everywhere, even in France. They are secret and with much power. We are helpless against them."

"Is this true?" Magdalene searches Jane's face.

"I think Mimi is right," Jane responds thoughtfully. "I think our priority is to find what they want and give it to Whittington. Then he will most likely disappear as quickly as he appeared."

Mimi speaks up again. "How wheel we find what he's looking for?"

"First we pray," Jane answers. "Then we look at my list, and we pray again until something clicks."

"Get zee list please, ma Jane." Mimi is anxious to proceed. "I think something may cleek right now. We wheel all pray to zee Virgin Mother and St. Theresa."

Mimi recites a French "Hail Mary" while Jane gets the list.

"Flannel pajamas, four pair underwear, four pair panty hose, grey suit, blue suit, two white blouses, one dark red blouse, housecoat, slippers, sneakers, pill bag, and toiletries bag."

Jane gets more specific. "I've listed everything in those two bags further down." She reads again. "A smoked fish, a box of truffles, an airline magazine, twelve pages of notes for my presentations, my prayer book and Bible, photos of Sean and Shakeeta for Magdalene...."

"Wait! Wait!" Mimi is on her feet. "Did you say photos?"

"Yes," Magdalene answers. "They're pictures of Sean and Shakeeta on their hiking trip through Southern France. I'm sure nothing is hidden in the photo envelope. I've looked at them several times, and I've showed them to everyone. I've even showed them to you, Mimi."

"Yes, I remember." Mimi loses some of her momentary enthusiasm. "I just thought since Hershey and I found zee clue in photos yesterday, perhaps there eez a clue in zee photos today."

"What photos did you find yesterday?" Jane turns to Hershey. "Did you find something important yesterday on the Internet?"

"I don't think this is the time," Hershey hesitates.

"We find pictures of Hershey," Mimi enthusiastically answers the question. "She was a singer with a band called..."

Hershey cuts her off. "Never mind, Mimi! I'm not even sure that's me. I mean, it looks a little like me, but I can't remember anything about singing and dressing like that. You know, I think we should just concentrate on the list for now."

Jane is concerned that Hershey is not forthcoming with information about her identity. She does realize from Hershey's stumbling explanation that a more private meeting is needed. Hershey is uncomfortable about who she is. This does not surprise Jane.

She moves the present attention off Hershey and back to the list. "We may as well look at Sean and Shakeeta's photos again. Perhaps Mimi has a good hunch about photos and clues."

"Maybe eet eez not a hoonch," Mimi whispers. "Maybe the Virgin Mary has answered our prayer. Perhaps Mary wants us to look at zee photos."

"Well, I hate to disappoint all you miracle chasers," Magdalene says sarcastically. "But it's impossible to see the photos."

Jane is annoyed at Magdalene's attitude. "Why is it impossible? I think we should look at them again, so we can cross it off our list."

"You never liked Sean, did you, Jane?" Magdalene slings her words across the room. "You never liked him because he's a scientist, and you equate that with medicine. You hate all doctors. Tell the truth, Jane. You only went to dinner with him because he insisted on giving you the photos for me."

Jane's mind is too full of Hershey's missing identity, government men breaking into their house, and a young Sister who believes in miracles. *Magdalene will not pull me into an argument*, she thinks to herself.

"You are correct, Magdalene. I never cared for Sean, not because he was a scientist but because he makes a secret out of everything. According to Sean, he flies from country to country at the drop of a hat to carry out secret experiments on cooking spray. Really! Can cooking spray be that important? I always felt he embellished his job for your benefit."

"That is a terrible thing to say!" Magdalene defends her family. "Sean works for a multi-national research company with government project grants. He has security clearance at the highest level. He doesn't travel like the rest of us, waiting in airports and taking off his shoes for inspection. He has access to a private jet. He just walks on, sits down, and travels around the world. Does that sound like he just works on cooking spray?"

"Oh yes, I forgot." Jane is overly-controlling her temper. "He also researches some kind of plastic to cover basketballs. I suppose basketball covers can take you around the world."

Magdalene's face contorts. Her breathing quickens and on every exhale her cheeks puff out like a bellows. "He does not make basketball covers!" she finally yells. "He's working on artificial leather!"

She quiets her voice and grits her teeth. "You will admit, won't you, that there is a need to replace leather with new materials, ecologically friendly materials?" She prepares a final volley. "You don't have any living relatives, do you, Jane?"

"No." Jane is repentant now, fully aware that she could have stopped the argument from escalating. "I wish I did have at least one living relative. I wish I had someone to be proud of like your nephew. I'm sorry, Magdalene. I didn't mean to disparage Sean or his work. I just think we should look at those photos."

Magdalene sits and lets out a loud sigh. She's exhausted but will not give an inch. "Sean called me last week. He lost the negatives to those photos and wants me to send him the originals. He needs to copy them. I have them all packaged and ready to mail. I've already applied the stamps. I simply can't justify ruining the package since we've already looked at the photos and the envelope they came in."

"Maybe Mère Marie wants us to look at them," Mimi offers meekly.

"All right! All right!" Magdalene dramatically throws her hands up. "I will get the photos, and I will tear apart all my time-consuming packaging. I just hope you are all happy viewing my private photos again." She stomps off to her room.

Jane takes this opportunity to address Hershey. "We will discuss what you found on the Internet later this afternoon. Will that be all right?"

Hershey makes eye contact with Jane. "Isn't it a coincidence that Sean asked for the photos back, now?"

"His request only seems strange because of our recent visits from Agent Whittington." Jane taps her finger on the list resting on her lap.

Magdalene stomps back and dramatically tears open the package in her hands. "I hope you're all satisfied! This package will now look like it went through a shredder!"

While Magdalene continues ripping open the package, Jane asks, "Don't you find it strange that Sean asked for the photos back?"

Magdalene, in almost slow motion, sits back on the sofa. The battle is lost. She tries to untangle her fingers from the sticky packaging. "If you must know all my private business, just ask. I will be glad to tell the whole world."

Everyone in the room looks at her in anticipation. She gives no further response.

"Well? Why does he want the photos?" Jane tries again.

Magdalene gives the package a last, mighty rip. The photos and a note scatter all over the floor. No one moves. "Sean needs these photos for a scrapbook. They have adopted a child from Sri Lanka. She is a special needs child whom no one wanted. She has several birth defects, but Sean and Shakeeta are very happy with their new daughter."

She relaxes her shoulders and calls off the fight. "That's why the photos are important. The scrapbook is for his new daughter, Gabrielle."

"Gabrielle eez a beautiful name," Mimi says.

Jane stifles her frustration. "Congratulations, Magdalene. You are now a great aunt." She smiles until Magdalene smiles back.

"I will personally help you repackage the photos," Jane offers. She gets down on her hands and knees and starts picking them up. All the others but Magdalene join in. The kneeling causes pain in Jane's leg, so Mimi helps her up while Hershey finishes gathering the photos.

"If you think it's appropriate," Jane ventures again, "we will include a congratulations card and a medal for Gabrielle. We can all sign the card."

Magdalene is calm and answers in her normal whiny voice. "He doesn't want anyone to know yet. The child is badly deformed. They want her to have some surgery before they tell anyone. He would have brought her here to see me if she was up to traveling."

"We wheel pray for her." Mimi breaks the awkward tension in the room.

Another round of "Hail Mary's" resonates in the room while Jane spreads the photos out on the dining room table. There are nine in all. The first four are of Sean and Shakeeta on a black checkered blanket having a picnic. The next five have them standing on a hill with the lush countryside behind them. The Sisters and Hershey are next to each other bending over the photos in front of them.

Mimi picks up the one in front of her. "Shakeeta does not look French."

Magdalene responds in a bothered tone. "She's obviously

African-American. He met her in Cleveland where they live."

"Oui." Mimi returns to the photos. "I know this area. Eet eez called, Lomage. Eet eez fifty kilometers from Paris and famous for goat cheese and tourists."

"Yes." Magdalene picks up a different picnic photo. "Sean explained how a goat herder passed by and offered to take their picture. He was so patient, Sean said. He even suggested they pose with the hills behind them."

Mimi continues to study the photo she is holding. Sean and his wife are in front of the hills. She brings it close to her glasses and then moves it away. She takes off her glasses. "What eez in zee sky?"

Hershey leans over and looks at the photo. "I think it's a plane, maybe a blimp."

Jane takes the photo and holds it below her bifocals. "It looks like a spaceship," she says nonchalantly. "The Sisters of St. Francis Dupre..." she answers Hershey's unasked question. "...have always been open to paranormal phenomena. One of our core beliefs is that God has created all things in the image of His love. We humans just don't always see with His vision."

"Your Order believes in spaceships." Hershey repeats the answer.

Mimi gently takes the photo and looks at it again. "You are right. Eet does look like zee spaceship. Spaceships have bean in Lomage before."

"Let me see that!" Magdalene pushes her way next to Mimi. "It's just a reflection of the sun, just a reflection from the camera facing the sun. Really, Jane!"

Each of them holds a countryside photo. Jane holds two, one in each hand. "It's not in any of these. No reflection. No spaceship."

"Eet eez here," Mimi says. "I think, there are zee flames too. Eet eez hard to see." She hands her photo back to Jane.

"It does look different in this one," Jane comments. "And that does look like a flame or smoke, something."

Hershey looks at the photo over Jane's shoulder. "I think it's smoke. It looks like the spaceship is falling."

Jane spreads out the three photos and then rearranges them. "There." She points to the set. "It certainly is falling. You can follow the descent in these pictures."

She leans closer. "I'm just not sure if that's fire and smoke or just exhaust like an airplane sky-writer. The sun is too bright to make out exactly what it is."

Magdalene elbows in and picks up the last photo. "I think it's a reflection from the sun." She squints at the photo and then demands, "Can we please all agree, it could be a plane not a spaceship, an ordinary plane with heavy exhaust?"

"If it's a spaceship," Hershey totally ignores Magdalene's comments, "that would explain why the International Intelligence Agency is interested."

"It is not a spaceship!" Magdalene starts picking up the photos. "I will not let you drag my nephew into something ridiculous. Something you may think is funny but could end up on the cover of some supermarket magazine. I am sending these photos to him right away."

Magdalene tries to grab the last photo out of Jane's hand. Jane won't let go. "You're right, Magdalene. Try to calm down. We aren't going to say anything to anyone. It's probably a plane."

Jane releases the photo, and Magdalene shuffles them together. Jane puts her arm around Magdalene's shoulder. "They are beautiful photos. I'm sure they will make Gabrielle smile. Please, let me repackage them like I promised. I'll do it right away. We've worked too hard this morning and with the incident last night, I think we all need to take a break from solving our mystery."

"You could be right." Magdalene hands the photos to Jane. "I need to go to the Thrift Shop and sort the new donations. Mimi, you promised to come with me."

Mimi smiles and nods, ready to work.

Jane organizes the photos. "I'll put these in a new envelope and personally take them to the post office." She looks at her watch. "They should be on their way to Cleveland by four o'clock. Hershey, you can help."

Magdalene is anxious to end any discussions concerning the IIA, suitcases, or spaceships. She is relieved to go to the Thrift Shop and perform some mundane routines.

Jane hunts through her newly organized desk and finds a mailing envelope. Hershey follows her into the office and cuts the postage off the old envelope. Together, they tape it to the new package, but Jane doesn't seal it. Nonchalantly, she says, "Before we get to the post office, I need to make a stop."

CHAPTER 12

Jane finds a parking space a block away from the Post Office. She hurries Hershey down the shop-lined sidewalk to the *Old Booksellers* and pushes open the wooden front door. A tinkling bell announces their arrival. The smell of old books and new magazines stir up positive memories for Jane who loves to read.

An elderly gentleman, sitting behind the counter pushes up his thick, black-framed glasses. "Good afternoon, Sister. How may I help you today?"

Jane moves to the counter. "Good afternoon, Mr. Roberts. Remember how you made that old photograph larger for me?"

Hershey notices that Mr. Roberts whistles as he speaks. This in turn causes his mustache to lift and wave with each word.

"I scanned it in and blew it up." His longish grey hair also moves up and down with his mustache.

"Yes, that's what you did." Jane smiles. "I wonder if you could make two other photos that large."

"That depends," he whistles. "I'll have to see the quality of the photos. My scanner isn't that sensitive you know."

Jane sorts through the snapshots in Sean's package. "These are the two I'd like you to make larger. Can you do it?"

Mr. Roberts looks at the photos and happily whistles, "Yep. Yep, I can." He pops up and exits into a back room.

While he's gone Jane and Hershey browse the rows of books and magazines. Hershey is drawn to *Behind the Alternative Scene Magazine*. On the cover is a green-faced teenager in a snake suit with three stud earrings pierced through his tongue. She opens to the *In the Groove* page. The third paragraph is highlighted. **Stink Couple Split**.

She silently reads the article. "Old history-makers, Sky Volta and Wolfgang Merge have called it quits. Wolfgang asks any fans who see Sky to tell her he bought the farm, and the kids need her. Looks like these two sexy rockers are now available. That is, if you can find them and if you like old."

The phrase, "The kids need her" gives Hershey a shiver. *What if she has children?* This thought puts a small ache in her heart. Maybe her children need her. Maybe they're looking for her and can't find her. What if her ex-husband wants to send them to an orphanage? "I can't believe that my marriage, which I can't even remember, is already over," she says to herself.

Mr. Roberts reappears and Hershey joins Jane at the counter. "These were a little tricky, but I got' em." Mr. Roberts waves the two sheets of paper.

He hands the enlargements to Jane and her eyes widen. "They're wonderful!"

He hands her back the originals. "That'll be $12.50 which includes tax, and if you like science fiction, I have a whole row of it in aisle two."

"No, thanks anyway." Jane counts out the right amount.

Hershey steps closer. "Can you pay for this too?" She hands Jane the magazine.

Jane glances at the front of the magazine then fishes in her wallet for more money. She quickly repacks Sean's pictures and walks the few yards to the post office, where she mails the package. Hershey, magazine in hand, trails behind her.

Jane looks at her watch. "Just four o'clock. I told Maggie the package would be on its way by four, and it is."

She looks up and down the street and then hurries Hershey back to the car. "We need to discuss what you found out about your identity." She starts the engine. "But please bear with me for a little longer."

She hands the enlarged photos to Hershey. "Please look at these and tell me what you see."

Now that the photos are larger, there is no doubt that the thing in the sky and on fire is an elongated, cylinder-shaped spaceship. She looks at Jane and answers. "It's a spaceship. It's exploding or falling. You can see fire."

Jane stops for a red light and turns to Hershey. "We can't show these to anyone. I think this is what that man from the IIA wants. I think these photos are very dangerous to anyone who has them."

Hershey's thoughts connect with Jane's. "Which means Sean is also in danger."

"Yes." Jane tries to put her fears into words. "I am afraid so, but I can't show Maggie. She won't believe me. I'm not sure what to do."

"Maybe you can call Whittington, now that you know what he wants," Hershey offers.

"I'm not ready to tell him I know about the spaceship, not just yet." Jane heads for home. "Tonight, I will pray about this whole matter."

She looks at Hershey. "I want you to pray also. We have another house meeting in the morning and with God's help, we can then tell Maggie and the others. If we need to handle it ourselves, we will know that too."

Hershey isn't really sure how these prayer messages are supposed to come to her. She'll just trust Jane.

Jane turns a corner and abruptly changes the subject. "I want to see everything you and Mimi found on the Internet. I also want you to explain why you bought that magazine." Jane doesn't take her eyes off the road. "Do you know who you are Hershey?"

Hershey also keeps her eyes glued to the road. "I think I'm Sky Volta or Mary Margaret O'Brien."

******

Evening prayers are rather lackluster. Samuel petitions for guidance in passing his exam. Magdalene prays for a night without intruders. Jane prays for peace throughout the universe. And Hershey hums the closing hymn in a counter- rhythm.

Dinner is also noticeably quiet. Mimi tries to lighten the mood by discussing the various pieces of clothing Magdalene and she organized at the Thrift Shop. No one is really listening.

Jane requests another house meeting after morning prayers. "To discuss the IIA situation and Hershey's identity search."

******

Jane whispers a little prayer for guidance before Hershey enters her office. They take their places next to each other on the sofa. "Mimi was very good with the computer," Hershey begins. "First, we searched for a missing senator's daughter. Samuel read about her in the paper and thought she might be me. I'm not her, but she has a tattoo like mine.

Jane's eyebrows go up. "Is it in the same location?"

"No, no," Hershey answers. "It's on her shoulder. We found some pictures of her, and she doesn't even look like me. But we got the address and phone number for Sister Manchu's Tattoo Parlor. So we have a lead."

"Sister Manchu." Jane is stunned. "There really is a Chinese Sister. I never should have doubted you."

Hershey gives a forced grin. "We didn't find anything in the obituaries or the missing person's links. But then Duane told us how to search songs."

She flips through the papers on her lap. "This is what we found." She hands Jane the pictures of the singers.

"Talking Trash." Jane tries not to be surprised by the name or the pictures. She takes off her glasses and moves the paper closer to her face. "The woman on the left does look like you," she says softly. "That's almost how you looked the first day I met you, the same pointy pink hair, and did you notice the earring?"

Jane hands Hershey the picture. "I didn't even look at the earring, but it does attach to her nose like you said." Hershey rubs the hole in her nose.

Jane takes the picture again and reassuringly pats Hershey's arm. "Don't be so sad. This is good news. This is what we've been waiting for. Now we know who you are. We know your name is, let me see...yes...you are... Sky Volta."

She turns to Hershey, "Does that name sound familiar?" Then she thinks, *With a name like that, it's no wonder Hershey Ghirardelli sounded right.*

"No." Hershey doesn't look at Jane. "I didn't even think the picture looked like me, but I do think Mary Margaret O'Brien sounds familiar." She hands Jane the band information sheet. "I think that might be who I am."

Jane takes her time reading the information before she comments. "So, you are Mary Margaret O'Brien. That's a lovely name." She looks at the sheet again. "And you are a famous singer who toured the world, and you owned a record company, and you have a ..." She searches for the proper title. "...business partner named Wolfgang Merge. That certainly gives us a lot to work with to get you back home." Jane finishes on a positive note.

Hershey looks pleadingly into Jane's eyes. "I dress like a weirdo. I call myself 'Sky', and I got married in a Goth ceremony in Ireland."

Hershey is near tears.

Jane tries to help. "That's just show business. That's what Mimi would say, and she should know. Her two older sisters joined a circus for several years before they both got married."

Hershey picks up the magazine and flips through the pages until she finds the *In the Groove* article. She hands the open page to Jane. "I'm divorced...with kids."

Jane hesitates. She is not prepared for any discussion of marriage, divorce, or children. Then she remembers this is her friend, the woman who saved her life. She reads the article and says, "They're looking for you. That should make you feel better."

"But I'm married and divorced!" Hershey takes back the magazine. "I have to get the kids, and I still don't remember this Wolfgang Merge. I don't remember any of this!"

"Don't worry about the details." Jane tries to be reassuring. "At least we have a name. You can trace it for more information. The marriage, divorce, might be a publicity trick to sell records."

"But what about the kids?" Hershey asks.

"I'm sure if you had children," Jane is on unsteady ground, "you would remember something about them. Mothers don't just forget their children."

"What if it's true?" Hershey starts to cry. "What if I left my children, and they need me? I just can't remember." She buries her face and sobs.

Jane takes Hershey into her arms. "There, there," she tries to console her. "I know this is difficult for you, not knowing who you were or are. But now we have a chance to get some answers."

Hershey tries to stop crying. "It's not just the darkness in my head. I just worry that I'm not a nice person that I'm some kind of freak. Maybe I'm bad. Maybe I did leave my husband and my children. Maybe I just ran away, but I really want to be a good person."

"You are good! You are a good person!" Jane assures her. "You will always be a heroine, no matter who you are. And you will always be Sister Hershey."

This brings a hesitant smile to Hershey's face as she wipes her eyes on her sleeve. "I'll call the tattoo parlor and the record company in the morning and try to find out how to contact this Wolfgang Merge." She gains a little more confidence. "If I can't find him at the record company, maybe I can call this magazine. I think Mimi will help. She's very good at detective work."

"That's a good plan." Jane gets to her feet. "I'd like to put off any more discussions about the marriage and children until you've made those phone calls. I think it will all be much simpler when you get more information."

Hershey is embarrassed by her display of emotions. "You're right; it probably has something to do with show business. When I find out more, maybe I'll remember more."

She hesitates and then gives Jane a quick hug. "Thanks, you're a good friend. I never feel alone when I talk to you."

Jane is now the one embarrassed. She used to be able to ignore these emotional contacts, to put them in some neutral context, not feel too deeply, but something is changing in her life. Something is surfacing that she pushed away a long time ago. She thinks perhaps it is love, not romantic love, but not just caring either. She's not sure if feeling love again is a good idea. Love stopped for her at a very early age. People just stopped loving her, people like her father, her mother, even her sisters.

Jane shakes her head and deliberately ends the thoughts she is not prepared to deal with yet. "Remember, Hershey, I still expect you to pray tonight about our other problem. I must have a plan by our morning meeting. It also has to be a plan that Magdalene will accept. That's not an easy prayer."

Hershey laughs. "I can't promise any answers, but once I've checked all the windows and turned on the outside light, I'm off to my bedroom for the pray-a-thon."

Jane helps Hershey secure the house, and they go to their separate bedrooms. Jane's first prayer is for Mary Margaret O'Brien. "Please Lord, help her discover her true self and don't make her life too complicated, if possible. Amen."

CHAPTER 13

Jane sees morning arrive through her bedroom window. "Life is a blessing," she cheerily remarks to the chirping birds. "Perhaps the answer to prayer is not an inward voice but a visual panorama of nature's beauty." This last observation is directed to a chickadee on her sill. He responds by shedding a small white feather which floats to the ground.

"Maggie always loved sunny spring days," Jane talks to herself. "I know that seems like a real contrast to her stern demeanor, but I can still remember when she balanced her severity with much more sunshine. She used to be the queen of the April Fool's Day pranks. She loved a good laugh. She just let that rigid sense of propriety and her inner fears overpower the fun-loving child inside her. That can happen to anyone, especially when your beliefs get tested with reality, or when the life you have freely chosen is looked down upon, or laughed at, or seen to be less than the norm."

Jane looks at the small white feather again and watches as the wind gently skims it across the lawn. "That's the answer! That's the answer to my prayers!" She heads for her door and eagerly swings it open. Magdalene is right there, hand raised, ready to knock.

"Maggie!" Jane is surprised by this sudden apparition.

"Jane," Magdalene answers at the same time. "I want to talk to you before morning prayers."

Jane opens the door wider and Magdalene moves to the straight-back chair by the window. Jane sits next to her and lets the morning sun warm her shoulders.

"Try not to interrupt me, Jane." Magdalene uses her familiar curt tone. "I want to get through all of this before I change my mind."

Jane says nothing but waits for what is to follow.

"I had an unusual dream last night," Magdalene begins. "The dream was very confusing. It was about Sean and airplanes, and men breaking into our house. It was unsettling."

"I'm sorry," Jane offers. "All this negative excitement must be…"

"Jane!" Magdalene cuts her off. "I asked you not to interrupt."

Jane stops mid-sentence, and Magdalene continues. "I dreamt about grandmother Myrtle. I've spoken to you about her."

Jane is about to respond but catches herself.

"Grandmother Myrtle never wanted me to become a nun." Magdalene studies the back of her hands. "She never spoke to me after my final vows. She died never speaking to me again." Disappointment and pain show in Magdalene's face.

Jane reaches over and puts her hand on Magdalene's hand. Magdalene flinches but doesn't pull away. "Grandmother Myrtle was devoted to St. George. There was a large painting of him slaying a dragon in her living room. She made a yearly pilgrimage to the Shrine of St. George in Montreal."

Magdalene drops her voice to a whisper. "They both spoke to me last night in my dream."

"Grandmother Myrtle and St. George!" Jane sits up straight.

"Yes!" Magdalene's own surprise is obvious. "Grandmother Myrtle said Sean is in danger and St. George repeated, 'Sean is in danger.'"

Magdalene gives Jane a quick, fearful glance and continues. "Grandmother Myrtle looked at me with those demanding eyes and said, 'Help Sean.' Then St. George clanged up behind her and repeated, 'Help Sean.'"

"I didn't know what to do. They were so real, so concerned about Sean. I asked them what I should do. How can I help him? And St. George gave me the answer. 'The spaceship has put him in danger.' Grandmother Myrtle pushed under his arm and added, 'You can help him, Mert. I believe in you. Help him!'"

Magdalene leans closer. "She always called me Mert. I don't think I ever told you, but I was named after her. I never liked the name Myrtle, so I chose Magdalene when I took my vows. But Grandmother always called me Mert." Magdalene momentarily loses herself in her thoughts. "Then the most extraordinary thing happened."

Jane fears this is more than a simple answer to her own prayer. She leans in and listens carefully for the rest of this cryptic message.

"Grandmother Myrtle touched my face." Magdalene puts her hand on her cheek. "She touched me, and I swear I felt her touch. She said, 'I'm sorry, Mert. I only wanted you to be happy. I thought you'd be happy if you were married. If I had known how happy your life would be as a nun, I never would have been angry. I'm so proud of you.'"

Magdalene stops to regain her composure. "Grandmother Myrtle is proud of me. She wanted me to be happy." Magdalene chokes back suppressed tears. "My grandmother loves me and always has."

Jane doesn't know what to say or do. "That was certainly an unusual dream."

Magdalene stops Jane again. "That wasn't the entire dream."

"There's more?" Jane is incredulous.

"Yes." Magdalene straightens her posture. "St. George had one more thing to say. He said I should ask *YOU* how I can help Sean. He called you by name. 'Your friend, Jane Dalton, knows how to save Sean. Ask her to help you.' Then the whole dream was over, and I woke up."

Jane is speechless, but Magdalene is relentless. "What does this dream mean, Jane?"

"I'm not sure." Jane fumbles for an explanation. "I'm not an expert in dream interpretation, but I think you needed to make peace with your grandmother."

"What else does it mean?" Magdalene probes. "I know you know something. I can always tell. Why is Sean in danger?"

The dream may be a coincidence, or it may be the answer to a prayer. "I think Sean knows something about the spaceship in the photos. That's why he asked for them back."

The gravity of Jane's voice frightens both women. "I think the IIA know something about the spaceship too. They may be watching Sean like they're watching us. I'm afraid they may intercept the mail and get the photos."

Jane needs to add, "The IIA broke into our house to find those photos. The IIA is above the law and that puts Sean in grave danger."

Magdalene does not protest but resolutely asks, "Are you sure it's a spaceship?"

Jane gets her purse and takes out the enlargements. She hands them to Magdalene. "It does look like a spaceship."

"You made copies of my pictures? Really, Jane!" Magdalene unfolds the pictures and studies them. She jumps out of her chair and starts for the door. "I have to call Sean and warn him."

"No! Wait!" Jane jumps in front of her. "They may have his phone tapped. I think we need to go there. We can try to beat the mail and warn him."

"Won't the IIA be suspicious? Aren't they watching us?" Magdalene asks. "Won't they just follow us there?"

Jane paces her small room. "We need to talk to the others and ask for their help." She moves to Magdalene. "This will all work out. I know we can help Sean. We need to have faith, and the others can help us with that too."

They walk together to the small chapel, preoccupied with their own thoughts and personal prayers.

******

A sleep-deprived Samuel calls the house meeting to order and requests another week free from house duties. His Advanced Pharmacology course is taxing all of his time and energy. Mimi and Hershey volunteer to share the chores.

Jane stands and clears her throat. "Magdalene and I need all of your help. A very serious problem has arisen." She chooses each word carefully. "We are concerned that Sean is in danger. We have sort of agreed that the object in the photographs is a spaceship." She takes a longer pause. "And we do not feel we can go to the authorities for help."

"Why can't you call the police, or the FBI, or the IIA?" Samuel asks.

"No, chère Sam." Mimi immediately speaks up. "Zee IIA cannot be trusted. No. No. You must not tell them about zee spaceship."

Mimi peaks everyone's curiosity, and Magdalene is the first to respond. "Why Mimi, why can't the IIA be trusted to know about the spaceship?"

Mimi bows her head. "Because they wheel make you go poof." This last word is emphasized with upraised hands.

Magdalene throws Jane a worried look. Jane turns to Mimi. "What do you mean, 'Make you go poof?'"

"They wheel make you vanquish, vaporate..." Mimi hunts for the right English word. "They wheel make you be no more, like Sister Culberth."

"She means vanish, evaporate," Samuel corrects Mimi's English. "She means they make you disappear."

Magdalene nervously pushes on. "What about Sister Culberth? What happened to her?"

Mimi becomes evasive. "Perhaps, I should not mention Sister Culberth. She eez my godmother. But perhaps I should be silent."

A familiar shiver kisses the back of Jane's neck. "Please, tell us what happened to Sister Culberth. We need to know everything if we're going to help Sean."

Mimi says a quick prayer to St. Theresa and in a barely audible voice begins. "Our Sister Culberth was born in Lomage. She was just a young girl when her mother died, and she join zee Sisters of St. Francis. Every Saturday, Culberth visit her ninety-year-old father. She bring back zee goat milk and cheese, sometimes zee yogurt."

Mimi stops and looks around at the circle of faces staring at her. Her lower lip begins to quiver. Samuel leans over and tries to be reassuring. "It's all right. Don't be upset. Your English is fine. What happened next?"

Mimi tries to move forward. "When Culberth eez seventy, her father dies. Many of us go to zee funeral, and zee town people have a breakfast. They serve homemade wine, and Culberth she drink too much. In zee car coming home, she tell us her father saw a spaceship, and she fall asleep."

Mimi gets into the story now. Her face is more animated. "Most of us do not bother about what she say. On zee next day, two men from zee IIA come to see Mother General. She call all of us who were with Culberth into her office to speak with zee men. They ask what Culberth told us, and Mother General gives us *Zee Special Look*."

"What's *Zee Special Look?*" Hershey interrupts.

"*Zee Special Look*." Mimi does not understand why the phrase is questioned.

"She means," Magdalene glares at Hershey, "*The Look* that means be silent. Really Hershey, haven't you ever had a mother who gave you *The Look*?"

Hershey gives a quiet, "Oh."

Everyone turns back to Mimi. "We say Culberth was sleepy from wine and tells us nothing, nothing of sense. They let us go back to our work. But when they question Sister Culberth, they make Mother General go from zee room."

Several gasps circle the prayer room as Jane, Magdalene, and Sam respond to this unacceptable behavior.

Mimi agrees. "For several weeks, we hear funny noise when we peek up zee phone. We see dark cars parked on streets by zee Mother House. Zee IIA men come back three times to speak with Sister Culberth. Mother General call zee Bishop. He call zee government. He even call Rome, but we are steel watched. Mother tells us nothing can be done. Culberth eez very sad that we are frightened."

Mimi's face reflects the sorrow of that time. She shakes her head slowly. "One day, Culberth does not come to morning prayers. She does not come to breakfast. We cannot find her anywhere. We call zee police and search for two weeks. She eez poof." Mimi again raises her hands for emphasis. "But eet eez not zee end of Culberth."

Mimi has everyone's rapt attention. "What happened?" Jane asks.

"What happened then?" Magdalene demands.

"Mother General gets a phone call from America in San Francisco," Mimi continues. "Eet eez from Sister Culberth. She say she eez leaving the Order and wheel no longer be a Sister of St. Francis Dupre."

Mimi pauses while everyone inhales in shock. "This eez why you must not go to zee IIA. Eet eez why you must trust no one and tell no one about zee spaceship. If you do, we wheel all go poof and end up leaving our order and living in San Francisco."

All fall into silence as the full weight of the story sinks in. Magdalene is first to speak. "We have to warn Sean. We may already be too late."

"The photos haven't arrived in Cleveland yet," Jane answers. "I think the IIA is still watching us. They probably think we have the photos. We can get to Cleveland before the photos arrive."

"But if they're watching us," Hershey offers. "They'll just follow you to Cleveland."

"Then we will *just* have to lose them on the way." Jane stands, ready for action. "I have a plan that needs all of your help."

All agree to help but Magdalene who waits to hear what the plan is before she agrees.

"Samuel," Jane shoots orders. "You are in charge of Mimi and Hershey. That should not interfere with your studies. Hershey, you and Mimi will follow-up with your identity search. Magdalene put on some old clothes and pack for an overnight stay. We are going to Cleveland. We'll drive to Canada first and stop at the Six Nations of the Grand River. I need to have a talk with Charlie Lightfoot."

"Charlie Lightfoot!" Magdalene is on her feet now. "He is nothing but a common criminal, a con man. Why are we visiting Charlie Lightfoot when we should be racing to Cleveland? Canada will take us totally out of our way. We'll lose hours if we go up there."

"We will hopefully *lose* the IIA if we go up there." Jane lets a sinister smile spread across her face. "I thought of Charlie this morning. A white feather floated past my window, and his name just popped into my head. Charlie can help us."

CHAPTER 14

Jane and Magdalene wear gardening jeans and matching "they-were-on-sale" jackets. They pack their overnight clothes in brown grocery bags and hurry out to Jane's car. Commuter traffic is still heavy as they hit the Thruway heading for Buffalo and the Peace Bridge to Canada.

Samuel takes his leadership duties seriously. He delegates house chores to Mimi and Hershey before he leaves for his morning classes. The chores take less than an hour to complete, so the two women are soon huddled around the computer printouts in Hershey's room.

"Why don't I call the tattoo place and see if anyone remembers me?" Hershey suggests. "Maybe Sister Manchu keeps records of her customers."

Mimi hands her the phone. "Eet eez a good start."

Hershey pushes in the numbers and hears a recording. A child-like female voice gives the following information, "Sister Manchu's Tattoo Parlor is closed until further notice. The owner, Heidi Manchu, that's me, and the beautiful Mary Claire Clary have moved to Massachusetts so we can get married. We love each other very much. I want to thank my customers for their patronage and always remember, your skin is the canvas for my art work, so take care of it."

Hershey hangs up. "The tattoo parlor is closed and Sister Manchu has moved to Massachusetts."

Mimi's natural curiosity gets the best of her. "Deed she say why she has moved?"

"She wants her customers to care for their skin." Hershey avoids giving the real answer.

"Caring for zee skin eez good, but what are you not saying, chère?"

Hershey blurts it out. "Heidi Manchu is going to Massachusetts to marry Mary Claire Clary. I don't think she can help my search."

Mimi double-checks her translation. "Perhaps the Wild One wheel settle down eef she eez married. Marriage was very good for my circus sisters, Claudette and Celine."

She moves her attention to the printouts. "Maybe now wheel call zee record company. Maybe they have a phone number for..." she carefully pronounces, "Talking Trashcans."

Hershey starts to correct the name but changes her mind. She picks up the phone and pushes in the numbers for MadNight Records. A perky female voice answers. "MadNight Records. If it's bad, it's ours."

Hershey clears her throat nervously. "I'd like to speak to someone who knows about Talking Trash."

"One moment please," the young woman sings back.

The next voice is deep and husky, an older man who spends too many nights drinking whiskey and smoking unfiltered cigarettes. "Hello. This is Jake Hammer. What can I do for you?"

For a fleeting moment, a familiarity clicks in Hershey's brain. She knows this voice. She can picture the tall, bearded giant with shoulder length hair. The phrase, "Jake the Snake" comes to mind. But in that same instant, this familiarity slides back to a hiding place in her memory.

"Hello? Is anyone there?" He is less patient now. "I'm a busy man, got no time for this crap." He coughs into the phone.

Hershey is afraid he may hang up. "I'm trying to get hold of Wolfgang Merge from the Talking Trash."

"Sky! Sky! Is that you?" Jake begins to laugh. "Are you in trouble this time, Sky Girl. Where the hell have you been hiding? Dave is super-pissed. You're screwed! History! What the hell happened?" He waits for a reply.

Hershey gets nervous and meekly repeats her request. "I need to get hold of Wolfgang Merge. Do you have his phone number?"

"Oh, so this time it's really bad!" Jake booms back. He betrays a tone of disgust and cuts her off. "You can't remember anything, can you? You smoked some really bad shit, washed it down with too much rubbing alcohol and short-circuited your brain cells didn't you?"

He almost waits for a reply but condescendingly adds, "You two could be real hot right now. You could be tearing your clothes off all over the world, gold coins just falling at your feet, but no. You just can't stay away from the mind-benders, can you? Well, I got better acts than you now. You're the old, the used-to-bees, the washed up has-beens. You screwed up your career and your marriage."

Hershey can feel his anger. She hears him turning pages and sucking on his cigarette again. "He's still on that little farm in Colden, New York. Here it is. You got a pencil and some paper? Can you write or is your hand shaking too much? You were always some piece of work. You wasted it all on pills and shots. You coulda been rich. Instead you're just another bum."

He gives two short coughs and continues. "The address is 407 Hilltop Road. The phone number is 716-555-0543. But don't be surprised if he's through with you. Asia Talbert's been spending a lot of time around Dave, and he ain't the type to wait too long. You know what I mean? You're dead in the water. Nobody needs a bum who dopes and drinks till she don't remember who she is. You need help. Now, I got money to make." He slams down the phone.

Hershey numbly holds the phone to her ear long after he hangs up. She tries to make some sense out of what he said, but it only adds more confusion. Mimi finally realizes the conversation is over and touches Hershey's arm. "What deed he say?"

Mimi waits for a moment and then takes the paper from Hershey's hand. "You have zee address and phone number. Eet eez good."

Hershey recovers. "Yeah. That's his number, but I'm not sure if I should call him."

"What eez wrong, chère?" Mimi is concerned about the change in Hershey's demeanor. "What have you found out? What eez wrong?"

Hershey rubs her forehead. "I think I'm a bum, a druggie who can't remember who she is." She looks at Mimi. "I'm not very nice, and I'm a has-been."

Mimi is professionally concerned. As a social worker, she knows the dangers inherent when a person with amnesia starts to discover who she really is. As a nun and a new friend, she is concerned that Hershey does not see her inner self as Mimi sees her. "Oh chère, you are a nice person." She touches Hershey's arm. "Why do you think you are a boom in zee past perfect? What has upset you?"

"This guy named Jake," Hershey hesitates. "He knew me, and I think I know him. I just can't fully remember. Anyway, he said I did bad stuff and drank too much, and left this Wolfgang or Dave, who can't find me, and some Asia is chasing him. I could be taking my clothes off all over the world, but now I'm a has-been."

Mimi tries to follow the whole explanation. She adjusts her glasses and thinks carefully. "Why do you want to take your clothes off all over zee world? And what bad stuff deed you do?"

Mimi's sincere interest brings Hershey out of her self-pity. "I'm sorry Mimi. I guess I did use a lot of slang. He meant, I did too many drugs and drank too much alcohol and ruined my chances of being a star performer. 'Has-been' means washed up, a ruined career, broke and forgotten."

"Chère Hershey." Mimi takes on a teaching tone. "I do not think washing up eez a bad thing. I also think you do not do drugs nor drink now. A forgotten career, from zee pictures we see...you were not Frank Sinatra."

Hershey looks at the pictures of Talking Trash and starts to laugh. Mimi joins in and the tension is broken. The telephone conversation is put into proper perspective. "You're right, Mimi. I'm not Frank Sinatra. I'm still not sure who I am, but if it's a has-been performer," she holds back another laugh. "Then I'll live with it, and as you say, keep washing up."

She looks at the address and phone number. "I have to find out why this man is pissed at me, and about the kids, if there really are any."

She picks up the phone again. "Maybe this is all I need to figure out who I really am."

She presses in the numbers and waits for someone to pick up. "Hello," an almost familiar woman's voice answers.

Hershey tries to be business-like. "Is Wolfgang Merge or Dave Hill there?"

"Is that you, Sky?" The voice asks. "Where the hell have you been? What's the matter with you? This time you really did it! You know how long it's been?"

Since she heard a similar accusation just minutes earlier, Hershey decides to interrupt this one. "Is this Wolfgang?"

"You know damn well it's not Dave. This is Asia."

Hershey gets more assertive. "Please put Wolfgang on the phone. I need to speak with Wolfgang Merge or Dave Hill."

"Not this time you don't," Asia fires again. "He told me that if you ever called I should tell you to go to Hell! He's not talking to you, and he doesn't want you back. You are splitsville. Dave has a legal divorce paper and everything. So, last half of *Talking Trash*, you just send us the address of the flophouse you're staying at, and his lawyer will talk to your lawyer."

Before Hershey can interrupt, Asia hangs up the phone. Hershey turns to Mimi. "His lawyer will speak to my lawyer."

"Eet eez *not* good," Mimi replies. "You wheel need to talk to this man without lawyers, to find out who eez zee real Hershey Ghirardelli.

"I agree." Hershey is bolstered by the task at hand. "I need to go to Colden and see this guy. I need to explain what happened to me and find out who I really am. And maybe I need to apologize for hurting him in some way."

Hershey stops talking. "I don't even remember getting married, let alone divorced."

They both study the picture of the two performers in full costume. "I need to go as soon as I can. And I want you to come along, okay?"

"Eet eez good," Mimi replies. "We will ask Samuel if we can go tomorrow. I know how to get to this Colden. Eet eez only a few hours from here."

CHAPTER 15

Jane sees a dark-green Lincoln weaving in and out of traffic behind her. It doesn't attempt to disguise the fact that it's following her car. "Jane, you're going too fast," Magdalene scolds. "Jane, Jane, too fast!"

Jane ignores Magdalene's protests and pushes the car to seventy. She watches the Lincoln through her rear-view mirror. "I'm doing the speed limit." She tries to see through the Lincoln's shaded windows.

When they arrive at the Six Nations of the Grand River, Jane pulls onto the access road leading to the reservation. The car following her stops at the sign declaring this sovereign land. It does not follow her onto the access road.

"They're not going to come on Native land," Jane tells Magdalene who turns to look at the parked car.

"I don't think Native land will stop them for long," Magdalene huffs. "They're probably calling another car to wait at the other end. When we leave, they'll just follow us again."

"Maybe," Jane says smiling. "Or maybe Charlie Lightfoot can find us a way to leave unnoticed."

"You're putting a lot of trust in a man who steals from church collection baskets." Magdalene stares out the window.

Jane shakes her head. "I explained all of that to you, Maggie. He was totally without money and thought the church money was for the poor." She pauses. "And that money should be for the poor, not the fuel fund or the roof repair or..."

Magdalene cuts her off. "How can you be so naive? Everyone knows how that money is used. A parish priest has to be a businessman, or we wouldn't have any churches. He can't take the collection money and distribute it to street people." She calms her voice. "I can't believe you talked Father Bronsky out of pressing charges. You bring this criminal back to our home and encourage us to listen for hours to his stories. Then you give him money for bus fare home. I'll be surprised if he's even here. He probably went to Las Vegas or something. I never did find that ten dollar bill I put aside for candles."

Magdalene stops talking. She realizes that Jane's concentration is on maneuvering the car down the poorly paved road. "Here's Skyhawk." Jane changes the subject by pointing to a corner street sign. "Now we need to find number 12."

"I'll help look," Magdalene grumbles. "But even if we find number 12, do you really think he lives there? Do you really think he gave you a real address? Why do I ever listen to you, Jane? We could be half-way to Cleveland by now. "

Magdalene stops mid-complaint and points to a small tidy cottage. A colorful totem is carved into a dead tree by the front door. A six-foot nine, swarthy-skinned man with silver-grey hair pulled back into a short ponytail leans against the totem. His long nose loses prominence as his penetrating brown eyes connect with the sisters. He smiles and waves.

"There's Charlie Lightfoot." Jane sees the welcoming figure.

"Did you call and tell him we were coming?" Magdalene asks indignantly.

"No. I didn't trust the phone not to be tapped. Maybe he's waiting for someone else."

Jane and Magdalene walk the short distance to Charlie's front door. He greets them half-way. "My dear Sisters, I welcome you to my home." He ignores Jane's out-stretched hand and pulls her close for a bear hug. He releases her and moves to Magdalene. She moves quickly out of reach behind Jane.

Charlie just laughs. "I've been expecting you for several days."

Jane stops in her tracks. "How did you know we were coming? We just decided last night, and we told no one."

Charlie looks down at Jane. "I saw you both in a dream, and I saw other things around you. You need my help. That's why you have come. I am pleased to help you, but first you must come in and rest from your trip."

He steps ahead of them and opens his front door. The two women enter a stark rustic den. One wall houses a rough stone fireplace, and the other walls are covered with hanging blankets, traditional leather clothing, and a large dream-catcher made of feathers and woven netting.

The room is devoid of furniture except for a hand-made rocker. The rough-cut branches of the frame still have bark on them. The seat is woven with the same material used in the dream-catcher netting. Charlie motions to a small pile of blankets close to the lit fireplace. "Please, make yourselves comfortable while I get refreshments. Coffee or something stronger?"

"Coffee is fine." Magdalene reinforces her propriety.

Charlie goes into the kitchen, and Jane tries ungracefully to lower her stiff body onto the blankets. It takes several tries before she finds a comfortable position. Magdalene stands, arms crossed, pointy nose twitching.

"I am not sitting on the floor." She uses a loud whisper. "I'd feel like some kindergarten student." She taps her foot impatiently and walks over to the rocker. She pulls it closer and gingerly sits on the edge of the seat.

Both women stare intently at the fire and barely hear Charlie reenter the room. He puts the tray on the floor and sits cross-legged next to Jane. He serves the coffee from this position.

"How can I help you Sisters?" he finally asks.

"There are some people following us," Jane diplomatically begins. "Government people who act above the law." She puts down her coffee. "What I'm trying to say is you may not want to get involved in this, and I will understand if you can't help us."

Magdalene knows the urgency of their mission and jumps in. "We need you to help us get to Cleveland. My nephew's life may be in danger, and we can't even go to the police!" She's shocked by her own desperation.

"I understand," Charlie says thoughtfully. "I can help you. My animal spirit came to me in my dream and told me what to do."

"Did he tell you we were coming?" Jane asks. "Is that how you knew?"

"Yes," Charlie starts to explain. "He gave me a vision of the convent-house, just as it was when I was there. But he showed me a black cloud moving among you."

"That was the robber," Magdalene interjects. "He broke into the house and frightened all of us. He practically tore the place apart."

"Yes," Charlie goes on in the same rhythmic voice. "He was looking for the photos. He wants the picture of the space bird."

Jane is surprised by these revelations. "How did you know that?"

"My animal spirit shows me many things," Charlie explains. "He is not always kind to me though. That is how I got in trouble in Syracuse. I went to your city to tell a friend of my vision concerning him. He was an Army buddy, Korean War. He was in the Veterans Hospital, and I had a message from his deceased father. I told him of my vision, but a nurse overheard our conversation. My friend died at the moment of hearing this message. Several workers at the hospital tried to keep me there. They do not believe in spirit messages. They thought I was crazy or dangerous, maybe suffering some trauma from the war."

"I ran away from the workers and the security guards. But when I reached the bus station, I was robbed of all my money even my silver ring. I was too proud to tell you that part. I am a big, strong man. I should not have been robbed. I was embarrassed and afraid to go to the police. I slept on the sidewalk that night in the doorway of an empty building. My animal guide was separated from me because of my pride, so I made a foolish decision to take some money from the church. That story brings us to this one."

"You should have explained all that to us." Magdalene realizes she judged him wrongly.

"Pride is a terrible thing." Charlie raises his hand for emphasis. "I am humble now. My path and my beliefs are clear to me. I am a smaller man, a happier man."

Jane knows they need to keep moving if they are to help Sean and his family. "Can you help us get to Cleveland without those men following us?"

"Your escape from those men is all arranged," he explains. "The plan was given to me in the dream. I will go too. You will ride in the back of my chicken truck. I will cover you both with empty feed sacks."

Magdalene has doubts about this plan. Her voice goes up a pitch. "Will there be chickens in the truck with us?"

"Oh yes," Charlie answers. "I am told to bring these chickens with us. Someone wants to see these chickens."

"But don't chickens bite?" Magdalene asks.

"My animal spirit spoke to the chickens this morning. They will not bite you," Charlie explains.

Magdalene and Charlie help Jane get to a standing position. Once upright, Jane asks, "What is the rest of the plan?"

"Two of my tribe's clan mothers will come to trade clothes with you. They will drive your car back to Syracuse and make many stops along the way: Niagara Falls, Batavia, perhaps Rochester. Their faces will be shielded. Their animal spirits are best as decoys. The dark men will follow them."

Magdalene throws Jane a worried look. "Don't worry," Jane responds. "We're in good hands. I feel the Spirit is at work here. We need to trust God and get to Cleveland."

Two grey-haired Native women enter through the front door. Magdalene protests that the women are too old to pass for her and Jane, but no one listens. Charlie mumbles something about "pride" and leaves the house to prepare his truck.

The women exchange clothes. Jane passes the car keys to the silent women and blesses them. The disguised clan mothers leave on their journey. Jane and Magdalene now both wear baggy overalls and red-plaid hunting shirts.

"Really, Jane! Is this necessary?" Magdalene sniffs the sleeve of the hunting shirt. "I don't think these clothes have been laundered. They have a rather musty smell."

"Maggie!" Jane's exasperation is apparent. "These are disguises. They are not meant to be fashion statements."

Charlie hurries them to the rusty 1990 Ford pick-up. He practically lifts each one into the back. He jumps up and shows them where they need to curl up. The four crates of chickens perform a loud chorus of concerned clucking.

"You can lie next to each other on that blanket. It will cushion some of the ride, but the backs of trucks are not made for comfort. After I put these feed sacks over you, I will put a few full ones around you.

He hesitates and looks at Magdalene. "Then I will let the two roosters free. No one will suspect that you are hiding in a truck bed with free-roaming roosters. They like to be out of their cages when they ride. It was also part of my vision that they will protect you."

Horror rushes into Magdalene's face. She turns to Jane, and then turns to Charlie. "How long do we have to stay like this with the roosters?"

"Until I am sure it is safe for you to come into the cab with me. It may be hours if they decide to follow me."

Jane reassures Magdalene. "We need to do this if we are going to help Sean." She pulls Magdalene down onto the blanket. "Cover us up please." She turns to the now-petrified Magdalene. "I'll start the rosary Maggie, and you do the response."

Charlie covers their feet first and then their bodies. The women start the repetitive litany of the rosary. Charlie is about to cover their faces when he remembers something. "Sister Magdalene?"

She stops praying and looks up at him.

"I just thought of another thing from the vision." He readies the final sacks. "Your lost ten dollars is behind your desk, caught on a nail."

Charlie finishes covering them and lets the roosters loose. He starts the truck and drives slowly. Unfortunately, the Sisters feel each bump in the road. He reaches the entrance to the Reservation with all the chickens clucking at full volume. He passes the parked Lincoln and keeps his meandering pace until he reaches Highway 403. Then he joins the fast-moving traffic and heads toward the U.S. and Cleveland.

Charlie searches his rear-view mirror for the Lincoln or any other car that stays behind him for too long. He drives at an even pace for two hours before he pulls into a Native American gas station. He's sure no one is watching and frees the now-jostled and bruised women.

Magdalene gets up first, and to her surprise, she is eye to eye with a dominant rooster. Not one to bear indignation well, Magdalene stares down the rooster until it walks away. She allows Charlie to lift her off the truck and waits for Jane to join her.

She brushes off her baggy overalls and addresses Jane, "I have decided that we will dedicate this trip to St. George. Please pray with me Jane, "St. George preserve us."

Jane puts her hands behind her back and tries to stretch herself back to her original height. Moaning from the stiffness and pain, she automatically responds, "St. George preserve us."

CHAPTER 16

Charlie weaves from the right lane to the left as he joins the bevy of Cleveland commuters making their way home from work. Magdalene is at the passenger-side window, acting as co-pilot. "Not this exit," she says sharply. "It's the next one. Let me see. I haven't visited in a few years and with all this road construction. That's it! That's the exit, Convention Center Stadium! You have to get off here!" She shoots the orders to Charlie who waits for an opening, crosses the two lanes and exits.

They leave the highway and Magdalene is in full command, directing the truck and its quiet chickens south on route seventy-one. They travel down several narrow roads with white farmhouses getting further and further apart, as acres of planted and fallow fields race next to the houses.

Charlie down-shifts for another steep hill as the truck mechanically groans. Magdalene yells and points to the top of the deserted country road. "There it is! That's Sean and Shakeeta's house."

The pick-up seems to be nearly out of breath as it makes the last climb. Charlie turns into the long gravel driveway and coasts up close to the farmhouse porch.

Shakeeta is standing on the long porch, but when Magdalene waves, she runs into the house. In less than a minute, Sean emerges with Shakeeta close behind. He heads toward the pick-up, and

Shakeeta runs to the red barn next to the house.

No one in the pick-up speaks or even moves. Everyone feels the fear and panic in Sean's expression. He goes directly to Magdalene, who rolls down her window. Before she can say anything, he yells, "You shouldn't be here Aunt Maggie! Why did you come? And why did you bring these people? I didn't ask you to come!"

Magdalene opens the door and steps onto the running board. She holds up her baggy pants so they won't get caught on her shoes and jumps to the ground. "I came to warn you!" she answers. "I came to tell you those photos put you and your family in danger."

"What do you mean?" Sean tries to control his anxiety. "I'm not sure what you're talking about."

Jane slides across the seat and jumps to the ground. She doesn't wait for Magdalene to respond. "The IIA came to our house and questioned me. They even broke in and searched for the photos."

Charlie steps down but doesn't join the two Sisters. He moves to the back of the truck and puts the two roosters in their cages. Then he lifts the four crates of birds down to the ground.

"I don't know what you're talking about." Sean protests weakly. "I don't know anything about the IIA or..."

Magdalene cuts him off. "I sent the pictures back to you before I took a good look at them. We raced here today to warn you. Men from the IIA are following those pictures. They don't want anyone to know about the spaceship." She swallows hard. "You're my family, Sean. I don't want anything to happen to you or Shakeeta and the child."

Sean nervously pulls on his right sideburn. He looks cautiously down the driveway and stares at Charlie who is leaning against the stacked crates. "Who's that man? Can he be trusted?"

Jane answers. "That's Charlie Lightfoot; he's a friend. He's helped us lose the men who were following us."

"Then you were followed." Sean panics and rubs his sweaty

hands on his jeans. "I was afraid of that. They have our phone tapped. I'm sure of it. I wanted to get those photos and destroy them before they found out."

He pulls his sideburn again. "We have to get out of here. We have to go some place where they won't find us."

He turns and runs toward the barn. Magdalene and Jane are right behind, their baggy pants flailing in the wind. Charlie slowly takes the top crate of chickens and follows the others.

Sean runs through the barn and out to a large penned area. He races up to Shakeeta. "They know she's here! We have to do something!"

Shakeeta is terrified. She grabs her husband and buries her tears on his chest.

Magdalene and Jane catch up to him. Magdalene gently touches Sean's shoulder. "We came to help," she says softly.

"There must be something we can do," Jane moves closer.

Shakeeta buries her face again in another spasm of tears. Sean looks at his aunt. "I knew they'd find out about the spaceship. I've worked for them long enough to know they get what they want and hide that information from the rest of the world. I just thought I'd have more time, time to make some plans, to find a safe place for Gabrielle."

Shakeeta sobs, "Oh, no! No! Not Gabrielle!"

Magdalene and Jane tighten their circle around the couple. "We still have some time." Jane tries to be reassuring.

"We will find a way." Magdalene stands tall. "St. George will preserve us."

This last comment draws Sean's attention to Jane and his aunt. "Oh my God! Now you two are in danger. Does anyone else know? Anyone who knows is in danger."

"Don't worry." Jane the General Moderator is in charge. "We have ways of taking care of ourselves. The other Sisters are not involved."

Magdalene throws Jane a disapproving look. Maggie never approves of lying. Jane justifies bending the truth in order to comfort Sean. She hopes what she's saying will become truth. For now, they all need to stay focused if they want to keep ahead of the IIA.

Shakeeta's fear suddenly propels her into action. She pulls away from her husband. "I'm getting Gabrielle, and we're leaving, right now."

She runs to the child's playhouse. Sean, Jane, and Magdalene follow. Next to the playhouse is Charlie's crate of chickens and a child-size tea table and chairs.

Charlie sits squashed into one of the children's chairs. Across from him sits a strange-looking little figure dressed in girl's play clothes. On the table is a yellow-tufted baby chicken.

Charlie and the child seem to be communicating though neither is speaking audibly. They seem to be discussing the baby chicken that the little girl is petting.

"Who is that?" Magdalene asks.

Sean and Shakeeta answer together, "That's Gabrielle."

Jane moves closer for a better look. The strange little girl is only four feet in height and very thin. Her head is noticeably larger than normal. She wears a long-sleeved blouse and small garden gloves.

Jane's attention is drawn to Gabrielle's head. It is of ill-proportioned size and appears to be covered with a latex-like mask. The mask fits loosely and has no real definition other than a poorly-formed smiley face. There are no eyebrows and no hair. The mask's eye-holes have fake lids and lashes. The entire mask appears to be an unfinished work in progress.

Jane is overcome with compassion. She realizes that the child's birth defects are extensive. She prays silently to Mary Mother of all and protector of children.

"Is he talking to her?" Shakeeta points at Charlie.

"I don't know." Sean shakes his head.

Gabrielle points to her parents, and Charlie turns to face them. "She says not to worry. She will go away, and you will be safe."

"No. No. We don't want her to leave." Shakeeta's voice is shaky and tearful.

"We'll go together," Sean interjects. "We can hide somewhere together."

Gabrielle moves around the table and takes Charlie's hand. Charlie stands and scoops up the young chicken. They both walk the chick to the crate.

Charlie stares thoughtfully at the mask and then turns to Sean and Shakeeta. "She says she loves you both very much, but it would be too painful if you were hurt. She will find someplace to hide until it is safe to return here or until her father comes for her."

Magdalene fights back her own tears. "Whatever we decide to do, we need to do it quickly." She turns to Sean, "I need to know everything about Gabrielle because she's coming with Jane and me."

Jane chokes back her emotions. "Do you really think that's best? Do you think we should separate the family?"

"I'm not sure," Magdalene answers indecisively. "But I know there is great danger here and not just because of the photos."

Sean wrings his hands. "When we saw the ship on fire and crashing, well, we went to the site and Gabrielle was the only one alive. We found three more, but Gabrielle started burying them, so we helped her. We hid as much of the debris as we could, but I know they found it."

Shakeeta continues the explanation. "Gabrielle was injured, but that wasn't the only reason we took her. She made us feel so calm, so loved. She's like a living miracle, a piece of eternity. Whenever she's near, we feel at peace. We took her to be our adopted daughter."

Sean puts his arm around Shakeeta. "I tried to make her a life-like mask because she looks so different from us. I just got started. I need to do a lot more work."

Everyone looks at Gabrielle, who is still holding Charlie's hand. Unexpectedly, a serene feeling of quiet and peacefulness comes over everyone. All the fear, the urgency, and the overwhelming concern leave.

Magdalene whispers to Jane, "There's something very spiritual about this child. We need to protect her."

Jane whispers back, "I don't think she will be safe with us. Remember, they're watching us. If the IIA..."

Sean finishes her thought. "If the IIA discover that Gabrielle came from the spaceship, they'll take her and do terrible things to her."

He has said what everyone fears. Shakeeta breaks the impasse and quickly moves to the house. "Let's pack and get out of here."

Everyone follows except Charlie and Gabrielle. Charlie carries the chicken crate back to the pickup. Gabrielle is right by his side.

Sean and Shakeeta are in the kitchen feverishly packing shopping bags and a cooler with food. Jane and Magdalene stand helplessly watching the frantic activity.

"Where will you go?" Magdalene asks.

"Where is there a safe place?" Jane adds.

"I don't know." Sean answers as he continues packing. "We thought this was a safe place. We'll just keep moving, maybe rent a trailer." He looks from Jane to Magdalene. "We have to save our daughter."

Jane takes the bag Shakeeta is filling. "Go and pack some clothes.

I'll finish this."

Shakeeta runs toward the bedroom with Magdalene following. "I'll help you pack. We can finish faster if I help."

They pack quickly and in unison. Magdalene is bent over the bed packing the small suitcase when she lets out a low moan and swoons onto the bed.

Shakeeta grabs Magdalene and tries to keep her from sliding to the floor. She yells for help, and Sean and Jane race to the bedroom. Sean helps lift his aunt's limp body onto the bed.

"What happened?" Sean asks.

"I don't know." Shakeeta is shaking. "I was handing her clothes. She was packing them. She just fainted."

Jane moves to the moaning Magdalene. "Maybe she needs some water or food," Jane searches for a reason for the collapse. "We did have a difficult ride here, and we haven't eaten in quite a while."

"I'll get some water." Sean hurries to the kitchen.

"There's a candy bar on the counter." Shakeeta follows him.

Magdalene is moaning louder, almost forming words. She moves her head from side to side fighting to return to full consciousness. Jane puts a comforting hand on Magdalene's arm. "Everything is all right, Maggie. I'm right here."

"Jane?" Maggie fights to open her eyes. She looks at the ceiling and slowly sits up. "I've just had a vision!" She speaks with wondrous fervor.

Jane sits next to her. "No, you did *not* have a vision. You're probably tired or just upset from all the excitement."

"I've had a vision, Jane!" Magdalene punctuates each word. "I should know if I had a vision or not!" Magdalene scolds. "Do you have to contradict everything I say?"

"We don't have time for visions right now." Jane is steadfast. "St.

George will have to wait until we get Sean and Shakeeta to a safe place."

Magdalene stomps to her feet. "Really, Jane! Are you belittling my beliefs?"

Jane turns back exasperated. "I am not belittling what you believe. We just don't have time for a vision."

"I'm going to tell you anyway," Magdalene stubbornly puts her hands on her hips. "I just saw the two Native women, who are wearing our clothes being put into a jail cell."

"What?" Jane is a surprised believer.

"I saw us in there too." Magdalene is less enthusiastic. "The cell was dark and dirty. It looked like the hospital you were in."

Jane moves closer. "That's just your imagination, Maggie. You're worried about what will happen. That's not a vision."

"I saw more," Magdalene is prickly. "I saw Charlie Lightfoot bring Gabrielle to our house. He left her there with...." Magdalene stops.

"Who? Who did he leave her with?" Jane asks.

Magdalene's face shows disbelief. "He gave her to Sister...to Hershey. Why would he do that?"

"I don't know." Jane hunts for an explanation. "Where are Sean and Shakeeta? They were just going to the kitchen. They should be back by now."

Jane and Magdalene hurry to the kitchen. No one is there. They give each other a worried look and walk out onto the porch. They scan the yard and the driveway. There is no sign of Sean or Shakeeta, or Charlie and Gabrielle. The truck full of chickens is gone.

"Do you think they escaped?" Magdalene whispers to Jane.

"I pray they did." Jane whispers back.

CHAPTER 17

Magdalene turns, takes a quick breath and freezes. Jane also turns, and now is face to face with Agent Edward Whittington. His tall well-sculptured body leans against the door frame, and he smiles broadly at the two women. He takes a few steps toward them.

Jane knew they would meet again, but she controls her growing fear by focusing on his out-of-character attire. Agent Whittington is not wearing a dark suit. He's wearing worn jeans and a black tee-shirt revealing strong, muscular arms and a well-defined chest. He is also wearing dirty sneakers.

Work clothes. Jane thinks to herself. *Dirty-work clothes.*

"Agent Whittington, what a surprise!" She tries to maintain some control. "What on earth are you doing way out here?"

Whittington gives a low I've-got-the-upper-hand laugh but says nothing. He just stares at the two women.

Magdalene now realizes who he is and her entire body begins to shake. She mentally repeats her litany to St. George and projects herself into her old classroom. This gives her back some of the control that is ebbing away into her fear. "So this is the man who broke into our house and frightened everyone."

Jane moves closer to Magdalene. The peculiar feeling in the pit of her stomach keeps telling her something bad is about to happen. "What do you want?" she finally asks.

Whittington takes a step closer. "You sure gave the boys the slip this morning." The smirk on his face finally fades. "We never realized those women weren't you until they stopped for lunch. Agent Brownstone sat at a table close enough to finally see their faces."

"How did you find us?" Magdalene calls on the courage of her patron saint and stands up to this dragon. "How did you know we were here?"

Whittington stares Magdalene down. "We have our ways of getting information."

"Those women didn't know where we were going," Jane says, questioning what he is saying.

"No they didn't," Whittington echoes smugly. "But Brother Samuel did." He waits for a response from either woman.

The women control their reactions. "He would never tell you where we were." Magdalene speaks evenly. "If he knew anything, he would never tell you."

"Oh, he didn't tell me," Whittington explains. "He told your old friend, Father Finnegan." He pauses and looks for a response.

"Did you know Father Finnegan once raised money to supply guns to Irish revolutionaries?" He doesn't wait for an answer. "When we reminded him of his past indiscretions, he was very willing to call Brother Samuel and ask when you were expected back and where was it that you went? Oh, Cleveland to visit your nephew, only a short visit. Samuel was more than cooperative."

Jane nervously takes Magdalene's hand and squeezes it to connect their needed courage. "Well, you've found us. Now what do you want?"

Whittington walks around the two women. This forces them to let go of each other's hands and turn to face him. He looks at the empty driveway and yard.

"We have the photos." He turns to them again. "They were right

Sister Amnesia
137

in the mailbox, very convenient. We also have your nephew and his wife." Magdalene grabs Jane's hand again and squeezes it harder.

He steps closer. "Where is the creature?"

Jane finds her voice. "I don't know what you're talking about."

"What have you done with Sean and Shakeeta?" Magdalene bravely demands.

Whittington stands to his full height, hands on his hips, voice controlled and strong. "I'll ask this once more, and you better think carefully before you answer. Where is the creature?"

Jane's anger is stronger than her fear. "I don't know what you're talking about."

"We don't know anything about a creature," Magdalene adds. "You have your photos now just let us go."

Whittington relaxes. He lets his arms fall loosely at his sides. "Maybe you don't know about the creature and maybe you do. I can't figure you women out."

He waves in the direction of the barn and a dark green car speeds toward the house. Whittington smiles malevolently. "I think we're about to find out just what you do know. Get into the car."

The women try to refuse, but two burly members of the Russian weight-lifting team leap from the car and run toward them. With perfect precision, the two gorillas stand behind each woman. Jane and Magdalene again disengage from their handholding.

The women are forced, at times lifted and carried, to the car. Magdalene is still struggling when she's shoved into the back seat. Jane is more resourceful. She flails her arms and uses her feet to keep the car door closed. But she's no match for the two men. One lifts her completely off the ground and the other forces open the door. One grabs her legs and the other pins her arms to her sides as they toss her into the car. Whittington, who is watching the acrobatics, slides next to Jane.

The two gorilla-men race the car down the driveway and onto the road. Jane slides closer to Magdalene to avoid touching Whittington but there isn't enough room. She hears Magdalene nervously pray, "St. George protect us...St. George protect us."

Jane joins with Magdalene's prayers. She studies Whittington's face, as he stares out the window. *He doesn't look evil, but what does evil look like?* She wonders.

******

After an hour-long drive down winding back roads, the Lincoln pulls into a deserted airfield. A small airplane, barely visible in the blackness of the evening, sits at the end of an equally dark runway waiting for its passengers.

The car pulls next to the plane, and the burly gorillas in one well-choreographed motion swing open the back doors. Whittington gets out, and the gorillas drag the now-less-resistant women to the plane. Jane and Magdalene are pulled up the stairs. The plane's small engines start immediately.

Whittington takes the seat nearest the exit. Jane is belted into the seat across from him, and gorilla number one sits next to her. Magdalene is pushed into the seat behind Jane. Gorilla number two buckles her seat belt too tight, and she has to gasp before he loosens it. He walks back down the aisle and leaves the plane.

Jane watches him from the plane window. She can see the car headlights move back down the road. The plane's lights flash on the runway and cut a narrow path through the darkness. As they lift off the ground, Magdalene bends forward. "Jane, are you all right?"

Jane disregards the gorilla next to her and unfastens her seat belt. She turns to Magdalene. "I'm fine, but how are you, Maggie? I know you don't like flying."

A long silence follows. "I think I'm going to be sick and then faint."

Jane gets up. "I'm going to sit with her." She pushes past the hairy-armed man.

He looks at Whittington, who nods okay, and he lets her pass. Jane slides next to Magdalene. "Try to think calming thoughts like a sea breeze blowing over a sunlit beach."

"We are flying in a plane that can barely hold us." Magdalene is nauseous and curt. "I don't like hot beaches. I'm very dizzy, and I keep thinking of Sister Culberth. I certainly hope we're not flying to San Francisco. I'll never last for that long of a trip."

Jane is about to suggest they say another rosary when the plane starts to descend. Magdalene lets out a long groan and wraps both arms around Jane. "Ohhh! Where are those little bags? Ohhhh!"

The first gagging sound sends Jane hunting for an air-sickness bag. Magdalene will not let go of Jane. The moaning and gagging last another two minutes while the plane descends. Fortunately, the plane is now rolling to a stop.

Magdalene feels the ground and relaxes her hold on Jane. It is totally black outside except for the dull lights on a long concrete-block building. The ground floor has a row of lit windows and two spotlights illuminate the entrance door.

"Come on!" The gorilla pushes the women down the aisle to the open door.

Whittington leads the parade with the two women obediently following. The gorilla is the rear guard. The presence of this massive guard keeps them from thinking about running away. They cross a short tarmac and enter the building.

The waiting area has an empty candy machine and a row of three broken chairs. There's a counter to the left which was once the ticket terminal for a small airport. The dust on the furniture, dirt on the floors, and all around cobwebs tell Jane it hasn't been used in years.

Whittington disappears down a hallway to the left, but the gorilla drags the women to the right. He stops at the first door and kicks it twice. A strange hump-backed man in his seventies opens the door. He wears a black pinstriped undertaker's suit with matching black tie highlighted with yellow paisleys. His face and hands also have a yellowish tinge.

He opens the door wider allowing a flood of light to escape into the hallway. The women are pushed into the room. It is empty except for a wall-length steel cage at the far end. Two folding cots and a large plastic bucket are in the cage. The only light in the room comes from an overhead metal-shaded bulb.

The gorilla pushes Jane and Magdalene into the cage. The Yellow Man turns a combination lock that holds the cage door closed. The two men whisper to each other and the gorilla leaves. The jaundiced man takes his position crouched on the floor by the door.

Magdalene starts to tremble. "Dear God! They're going to torture us!"

"Calm down." Jane tries to overcome her own panic. "They're just trying to frighten us. We have to be calm. We have to be brave." She leans closer and whispers. "Think of Sean and Shakeeta. Think of Gabrielle."

Magdalene shoots a quizzical look at Jane and leads her to one of the cots. She speaks softly, so the Yellow Man can't hear her. "Is Gabrielle a child or is she something else?"

Jane grabs both of Magdalene's arms as if she's about to shake her. Still whispering, she says, "It doesn't matter. Gabrielle is just Gabrielle, and we must protect her. They are not going to let us go even if we tell them everything they want to know. I think it's wise to keep our story the same. They have Sean and Shakeeta, but I don't think they found Charlie."

Magdalene nervously asks, "What is our story? I'm so frightened, I can't even think straight. Do you think they're going to...to...kill us?"

Jane doesn't know how to answer. She tries to put a story together. "We can tell them we were worried about Sean. We figured out that Agent Whittington wanted the photos. We can say, we were afraid Sean might lose his job. That's why we went to warn him."

"What about Gabrielle?" Magdalene clenches her teeth. "What should we say about her?"

"If they don't mention her," Jane warns, "say nothing. If they know about her, tell them the truth as we know it. Gabrielle is a special child from Sri Lanka. She hasn't arrived yet, but she will be adopted by your nephew and his wife. Gabrielle is a gift of God."

"But is she?" Magdalene asks.

"Of course she's a gift of God!" Jane reprimands. "How can you even ask such a thing, Maggie? We are all gifts of God."

Magdalene tries a little humor. "Even that guy?" She points to the crouching guard.

"He's some mother's son," Jane says dryly.

Two loud kicks on the door make Jane and Magdalene cling to each other. The yellow guard opens the door to the burly gorilla. They move toward the cage. Yellow Man twists the combination lock and swings open the door.

"You!" He points to Jane. "Come here." His voice is high and crackly.

Magdalene starts screaming, "No! No! Nooooo! Don't take her! Don't hurt her! Take me! Take me!"

Her tears and pleading are to no avail. The guard flits into the cell, grabs Jane and pulls her out to the awaiting embrace of the gorilla. He quickly locks the cage, and Jane yells to Magdalene, as she's carried out of the room like a sack of potatoes. "Don't be afraid, just pray!"

Once in the hallway, Jane is allowed to walk on her own. She can still hear Magdalene's cries as the Gorilla Man escorts her to another concrete room. The door is already open, so she's shoved in and the door is slammed behind her.

This room has the same bare-bulb lighting plus a desk and two chairs. Whittington sits behind the desk. He leans his elbows on the dusty top and motions for her to sit across from him. Jane walks slowly and sits down.

"You look tired, Sister." He sits back in his chair. "Probably hungry, too."

Jane says nothing, so he continues. "All we want is the location of the alien."

Jane controls her anger. "What happens to us once you get your information?"

He sits upright. "You don't have to worry about that. You'll be safe. We aren't murderers, you know."

"I'm not sure what you are, Agent Whittington," she replies calmly. "But I am sure you didn't answer my question. What will happen to us?"

"I'm not going to lie to you." Whittington takes a different tact. "You know about the spaceship. We can't have you frightening the American public with that information. You'll be resettled; you'll like it there...lots of people your own age. It's a nice town in a sunny environment."

"I don't want to be resettled." Jane makes every word crisp. "I have no intention of telling anyone what I saw in that picture."

"We can't take a chance on that." Whittington stays calm. "We can make this easy, or we can make it hard. The choice is up to you."

Jane's mind works overtime. She hunts for a way out for herself and Maggie. She remembers the mental hospital so many years ago. The best way to deal with her attendants was to give them anything they wanted or at least make them think she was cooperating. She studies Whittington again wondering if it will work on him.

"All right," she says. "I'll tell you everything I can remember. We didn't know about the spaceship until you kept looking for something I brought back from France. When Maggie and I saw what was in the photo, we felt we should warn Sean about you. We were worried that his secret research job might be compromised. That's why we were helping him pack when they disappeared. No one said anything about an alien."

Whittington listens intently. "You didn't see anything else or anyone else when you arrived at the farm?"

"No," Jane lies confidently.

Whittington gets up and walks to Jane. "What about those little clothes you were helping to pack? Who were they for?"

Jane remembers the hospital attendants. She told them the thought of alcohol made her feel sick. She couldn't stand the thought of drinking again. She remembers every cell in her body wanting to absorb the whiskey they poured into the paper cups to test and tease her. She would just keep saying it made her sick, couldn't stand the smell. Jane just tried to believe her own lies until they took the alcohol away and stopped playing the game.

She measures her words carefully. "Sean and Shakeeta are adopting a special-needs child. They already have some clothes for her. She will be a special gift of God." Jane looks at Whittington. She hopes he will stop teasing, stop the game.

He sits at the edge of the desk. "I can't figure you out Sister. I went to Catholic school. I knew a lot of Sisters. They were all pretty much alike, but you're different. I can't quite put my finger on what makes you tick, but I will."

He pauses. "I was even an altar boy. Do you believe that?"

"No," Jane counters. "I can't believe that someone who was raised to believe in God could end up like you."

Whittington forces a laugh. "That's what I'd expect you to say. Maybe I do have you figured out." He takes out his cell phone. "I want you to call your house. Tell the others that you've been delayed. You don't know when you and Sister Magdalene will return, but you will keep in touch."

He hands her the phone as he adds, "We don't want anyone calling the police yet. We need some time to make the arrangements."

Jane reluctantly takes the phone and pushes the familiar number. "Hello, Sisters of St. Francis." It's Hershey and her voice is very sleepy.

Jane wants to scream for help, but she knows she must not involve the others. "Hershey, this is Jane." She stays calm.

Hershey is wide-awake now. "Jane, are you okay? Is everything all right?"

Jane doesn't want Hershey to say any more. She quickly gives her speech. "We are fine. We just got delayed. Our visit is longer than we expected, and I will keep in touch. Good-bye."

Hershey cuts off the goodbye. "Jane, wait. I have to ask your permission for me and Mimi to go visit Wolfgang Merge. He won't talk to me on the phone, and I think I should go see him. I think it will help me remember."

Whittington is listening in on the conversation. Jane looks at him, and he signals her to answer. "Of course," Jane says. "You and Mimi have permission to go. And Hershey," Jane speaks quickly. "Take care of things for me please. Be in charge of any mail, packages or guests that come to the house. Will you do that for me?"

"Sure," Hershey answers innocently. "Sure, I'll take care of business. See you soon. Bye."

"God bless you." Jane hands the phone to Whittington.

"Very good." He puts the phone back into his pocket. "You can go back to your cell now. I'll see you get some food after I talk to Sister Magdalene."

The gorilla enters and is about to grab Jane's arm, but she shrugs him off and walks out of the room. She tries to calm Maggie before he takes her for questioning. "Don't be afraid," she tells the wide-eyed Magdalene. "He won't hurt you. He wants to ask some questions."

She gives Magdalene a hug and whispers in her ear. "Tell him the story we talked about. We don't know about aliens. The adopted daughter didn't come yet."

Magdalene, body stiff as a frozen cod, walks proudly out of the cage and into the hallway. Yellow Man locks the cage, and Jane prays to St. George for Maggie.

******

In less than twenty minutes, Magdalene comes marching back. The gorilla is three steps behind her and carries two brown lunch bags. She takes the bags from him and throws a schoolteacher look to Yellow Man. He obediently unlocks the cage, and she walks in with her head high.

"We have some food, Jane." She hands a bag to Jane. "Please say grace."

Jane haltingly prays. "Thank you Lord, for this food."

Magdalene pretends she is totally absorbed in the sandwich. "I told them about the photos and my concern that Sean might lose his job. I also said the new baby didn't arrive yet. I think he believed me. You know how I hate to lie."

Jane smiles and bites into the sandwich.

CHAPTER 18

Samuel is overly preoccupied as he leads morning prayers. He drags them out longer than usual. He asks Mimi and Hershey to postpone breakfast until after the house meeting. The three of them move into the living room where Hershey sits at one end of the sofa, and Mimi sits in the middle. This leaves the other end for Samuel.

"He, however, doesn't sit. He fidgets with his curly hair and paces the room. He opens the meeting with another long prayer asking for guidance in what he is about to say.

Hershey is concentrating more on Samuel's raven hair and deep green eyes than the prayer. She hasn't yet told anyone about her late night phone call from Jane, but she finally loses patience with this new round of long, redundant prayers. "Jane called last night, around three in the morning."

Samuel stops mid-stanza, and Hershey goes on, "They're both okay, but they won't be home for awhile. Jane will call back and fill us in on what's happening."

"I don't like zee sound of zat," Mimi quietly comments.

"Why, Mimi?" Samuel takes off his horn-rimmed glasses and totally loses track of his planned talk. "What do you think is wrong?"

"I believe..." Mimi shakes her head. "I believe ma amie Jane and Magdalene are in zee trouble. I believe they are captured by the IIA."

"I don't think so!" Hershey jumps in. "Jane sounds fine. She even said we have permission to go find Wolfgang. She told me to take care of business for her while she's gone."

"Then maybe she is in trouble." Samuel sits next to Mimi.

"What do you mean?" Hershey asks. "How does that mean she's in trouble?"

Samuel looks at Hershey. A long, no-words-spoken moment follows. He forces his glance back to the coffee table and tries to explain.

"Jane should have said, 'Tell Samuel to take care of business.' That's how the Rule works. I have to be in charge when she's gone."

"What exactly deed Jane say, chère Hershey?"

Hershey now joins the group concern. She carefully relays what she remembers. "She said to take care of any packages that come. And let me think, something about taking care of any visitors or guests that come to the house. That's the business she was talking about."

"Maybe eet eez zee code," Mimi says to Samuel.

He jumps up. "Of course! Jane's giving us a coded message. We're supposed to expect some visitor, and he or she will have a package."

He sets his jaw like a stern commando. "We can't tell anyone about Jane's message. If they're in trouble, someone may also be watching us. We need to be prepared for whatever guest or delivery comes, and whatever he or she brings."

Another long moment passes. Hershey worries about the Rule she just broke. "I'm sorry, Samuel. I didn't mean to interrupt your prayer. I got excited about Jane's call. I hope you understand? What were you about to announce?"

Samuel is less religiously dramatic than earlier. He walks to the front of the room and takes a deep breath. He can't look directly at Hershey or Mimi. His eyes are fixed on the formal photograph of the Foundress of the Sisters of St. Francis Dupre, Mother Maria Honora

Seraphina Scholastica. "I have something regrettable and important to say to my community."

Mimi coughs to get Samuel's attention. She follows by raising her hand. "I am so sorry to break up zee speech, but most of our community eez not here. The big cheeses are absent."

Samuel's tense shoulders relax. He again allows himself to be distracted from his troublesome announcement. He puts his hands on his hips. "Mimi, where did you learn that phrase 'big cheeses'?"

"Chère Hershey calls Jane and Magdalene the big cheeses," Mimi innocently responds.

Samuel looks at Hershey. "We will speak of our two Sisters in our leadership group with respect."

His stern façade softens. "I want to tell this to you two first." He is barely audible. "I'm going to leave the house and the community."

Hershey can't control her response. "What?"

Mimi's mouth drops open. "Mère Marie."

"I know. I know." Samuel pushes another curl away from his face. "I struggle with this decision every day, every moment. I have for weeks. I don't think I'm cut out for all the rules and regulations anymore. I tried to handle everything with prayer, but I can't."

He sits down between the two women and looks dejectedly at the rug. "I quit my job at the hospital. I can't agree with their policies."

"Do you want to tell us what happened?" Hershey tries not to intrude.

Samuel hunches forward and plays with the gold Army ring on his finger. "The hospital won't allow anyone in if they don't have insurance."

Samuel twists the ring again. "They turned away two homeless men yesterday. The hospital representative told them to go to the county clinic across town."

He sits up straight and angrily adds, "Those men needed medical attention right away. Our hospital wouldn't let me help them, wouldn't even let me give them a glass of water, so I...I quit. I ran after them and took them to the clinic in our car."

"Are there any other of zee policies you don't like?" Mimi asks.

"I'm questioning the abortion issue," Samuel says meekly. "I've seen terribly deformed babies who spend their lives on machines, and babies who are beaten, even murdered, by parents who won't give up 'their property' for adoption."

Mimi gives no response.

"I guess it's not just the policies but the hypocrisy of the hospital's mission. This was a Catholic hospital founded on love and charity. Those values are gone."

He takes a breath. "I wanted to discuss all aspects of my decision with everyone, but I don't see myself changing my mind. I prayed about what the Church teaches and what I really believe. The two don't always agree. I prayed a lot, and my beliefs didn't change. So I will leave. I finish my Nurse Practitioner course in two months. Then I can get a good job and pay back the Sisters for my school expenses."

His voice is calm. "I need to leave because I can't agree with everything we're supposed to believe. I've started to question some of our vows and Rules too."

He gets up to leave. "I'm finding my personal feelings are sometimes stronger than things like poverty and chastity, and I can't keep humility and obedience when I see injustice."

He walks toward the stairs but turns back. "I'll be home all day, so I can watch for the package or meet the visitor. You two can go see Wolfgang Merge." He gives Hershey a half-smile. "Maybe he has some answers for you, Hershey. I hope so."

Mimi mouths a silent prayer before turning to Hershey. "We need to start zee day. Jane and Magdalene will know how to comfort

Samuel when they return…if they return."

******

The smell of Mimi's homemade muffins fills the kitchen. Hershey is busy whisking several eggs in the silver mixing bowl when she says, "There's something I need to tell you Mimi."

Mimi abruptly stops buttering and apprehensively asks, "You are not leaving zee Sisters too, Chère Hershey?"

Hershey smiles. "I'm not really one of the Sisters, remember?"

"What troubles you, chère?" Mimi asks. "Eez eet zee trip we take to Colden?"

"No. That isn't my latest worry." Hershey studies the eggs again. "Something is bothering me, this feeling I have."

She looks up again. "For days now, I've wanted to, I just keep thinking about Samuel. I want to hug him not like we usually hug. I mean, I want to hold him. I actually, I think I want to kiss him. Do you know what I mean?"

Hershey is embarrassed and flustered. "What's wrong with me, Mimi?"

Mimi smiles knowingly and returns to her muffins. "Nothing, eez wrong with you, chère Hershey. You are just feeling frisky. Eet eez natural."

Hershey is confused. "I don't think this feeling is very natural. I really want to kiss Samuel, and he's our Brother. I've tried to pray this all away, but it isn't going. I don't understand. Is it my mind? Am I crazy or something?"

Mimi tries to help her friend understand. "You are *not* crazy. You forgot zee memory, but eet comes back. That eez why you want to kiss Samuel. You remember romance from your other life. You are okay."

Hershey rubs her temples and disjointed memories. Some past knowledge flashes in and out. She begins to know parts of herself

Sister Amnesia
151

again. "Romance?"

She grins and moves toward the cupboard but stops mid-way. "So, I can kiss him?"

Mimi smiles again. "No chère, he is not available to you, not now. He has taken initial vows and like me, eez for now married to Christ. If Samuel decides to become a priest or even remain zee Brother, there is no kissing and no zex. Zee marriage to Christ makes zex forbidden. We accept our choices happily."

She pauses. "I think maybe you remember a part of who you are. Eet eez good, but we must eat breakfast and go to Colden to find out who zee rest of you eez."

Hershey feels something in her psyche waking up. She is remembering. Her mind races backwards and forward, images and thoughts separating and finally colliding. She still wants to be in Samuel's arms, but for now she finishes cooking the eggs.

*****

Over breakfast, Hershey tries to verbalize her expectations for the trip. She needs to ask Wolfgang if they are married or divorced. She needs to know about the kids.

Mimi suggests they "Go with zee open mind and heart."

Hershey agrees that with all the blanks in her memory, "It will be best to deal with events when they occur."

By the time they are ready to leave, both feel eager to see what lies ahead, and both are eager to forget the "kissing" discussion.

CHAPTER 19

Colden, New York is located about four hours from Syracuse. That gives Hershey four hours to feel the butterflies in her stomach playing volleyball with each other. The landscape of green hills is dotted with small farms keeping a polite distance from each other, and the modern-looking suburban houses start changing into more traditionally rustic homes.

Mimi drives the other car, the old grey Chevy, slowly up the ascending hills. Hershey acts as navigator checking the map on her lap, the road signs and street names.

"That should be Hilltop just ahead." She points to the left.

Mimi slows down, and they both crane their necks to read the sign. "Eet eez Hilltop." Mimi turns the car onto the narrow country road. She drives another mile and stops the car. "Look at zee big heel." She points straight ahead.

Hershey looks up from the map and sees the steep incline that keeps going until it's lost in a mountain-top of trees. "Do you think this car can make it up there?" she asks.

"We see." Mimi pushes in the clutch and shifts expertly to second. The car moans and then starts to vibrate. They move slowly with Mimi never changing gears. The thick foliage hides some of the road as they climb higher.

The Chevy creaks and whines until they finally reach the summit.

Here the road levels off into acres and acres of meadows and natural woods. The vastness is breathtaking, and Mimi joins Hershey in admiring the natural panorama that surrounds them.

"Chère Hershey, I see no houses, no address numbers," Mimi finally says.

Hershey pulls away from the natural beauty surrounding them. "Maybe the houses are further up the road."

Mimi shifts and guides the car along the narrow hilltop road. They travel a few miles and Hershey sees a small house and barn cut out of a patch of woods. Mimi maneuvers the car as close as possible to the house which is set on a small hill above the driveway. The two-story pinkish-painted structure looks like a gingerbread house. The carved green shutters and scalloped eaves give it an Austrian chalet look. Several yards away on another small hill is a matching pink mini-barn.

Mimi parks next to two Harley-Davidson motorcycles and a muddy all-terrain vehicle. They get out of the car, and Mimi slips off her glasses letting them dangle on their gold chain. She straightens her white blouse and slips on her grey blazer. Hershey nervously brushes at the jeans she's wearing and also puts on her grey blazer.

Twelve steps have been cut out of the hill and are paved with flat stones that lead up to the front door. Hershey stops just before the door landing. "I don't think I can do this."

Mimi touches her arm and quietly says, "Eet eez okay, chère Hershey. We seek the truth. God eez with us."

Hershey isn't so sure. She doesn't recognize the house, or the barn, or the motorcycles for that matter. She steps up and pushes the bell. They wait but no one answers. Hershey rings the bell again. Finally, they hear loud footsteps.

A six-foot-tall Amazonian woman with bright white, spiked hair, wearing a black leather bra and leopard silk bikini underpants opens the door. "Well, holy crap!" she booms through her black-lipsticked mouth. "Look at who the hell is here!"

She turns and stomps back into the house. "Dave! Dave! You gotta see this!"

She's out of sight when Mimi leans into Hershey. "Do you recognize zee woman? She looks maybe like a Talking Trashcan, no?"

Hershey shakes her head. "I don't recognize anything. This place feels a little familiar, but I can't really remember anything."

Just then, a handsome man in his late twenties opens the door wider. He is about five-foot-eight and also wears black lipstick and black eye shadow, but his features are softer. His red hair is short and curly but not spiked. He's barefoot and wears jeans and a short top. His exposed navel sports two piercings, identical diamond studs.

He throws Mimi a quick hard look and then glares at Hershey. "Where the hell have you been?"

Hershey's eyes close as she rubs her painful temples. She tries to hold back a wave of dizziness and grabs the door frame to steady herself. Mimi quickly takes her arm. "Are you okay?" Mimi asks.

"Look at me, you useless waste!" The man in the doorway continues to scream into Hershey's face. "Don't think you can pull that 'I don't remember anything' crap again."

Hershey continues to massage her forehead. She whispers to Mimi, "I feel like I just got hit on the head. My heart is pounding. I need to sit down."

She slides down to the wide stone step while Mimi steadies her into a sitting position. Hershey's eyes are closed, and she covers most of her face with her hands.

"Speak to me, chère Hershey," Mimi says softly. "Are you okay? Do you need zee help?"

Hershey does not respond. She finally lets her hands drop into her lap and half-opens her eyes. "I'm fine Mimi." She sounds exhausted. "The pain is going away, and I'm fine."

Mimi's helps Hershey get up, and they face the less than patient man still planted in the doorway. Hershey does recognize his face...his voice...a past that recently hid behind a mental curtain. The blackness in Hershey's mind lifts like an early morning fog and in a very calm and worn voice she says, "Hello Wolfgang."

She turns to Mimi. "I remember Wolfgang and this place. I even remember some of the things that happened."

"Crap! Crap! And more crap!" Wolfgang screams again. "You should get an Academy Award. Now get your ass in here and bring your little girlfriend with you. We have some business to talk about."

Wolfgang stomps back into the house, and Hershey and Mimi follow. They walk down a dimly lit hallway and enter the living room. Mimi takes a look around and gasps. The floor is covered with old pizza boxes, fast-food bags and dirty clothes. Bras and panties are draped over the top of the fireplace and Styrofoam containers with rotting leftovers decorate a large sofa, chairs and tables.

A music video blares from a forty-inch television screen in the middle of the room, and empty beer bottles are lined up on the fireplace and in evey corner.

"I see you're still as tidy as ever," Hershey says.

"You should talk!" Wolfgang lights a cigarette and points it toward Mimi. "What are you doing now, picking up librarians?"

"She's a nun." Hershey answers matter-of-factly.

"A nun!" Wolfgang chokes on his cigarette smoke. "You should be ashamed of yourself."

"That's disgusting!" The giant woman enters from the kitchen. She now wears jeans with her leather bra and splashes a trail as she gestures with her beer bottle.

"Never mind!" Hershey ends the discussion. She removes the garbage from one of the chairs, so Mimi can sit down.

"I guess we do need to talk." Hershey looks from Asia to Wolfgang. Then in one sweeping gesture pushes the garbage to one end of the sofa and sits down.

"We need to talk all right." Wolfgang sits on the leftover food containers on the table in front of Hershey, demanding Hershey's full attention by moving within three inches of her face. He takes another long drag on his cigarette. "Where were you?"

Hershey stares back at him. She touches the fresh scar on her forehead. "I got drunk after that fight we had…you know, the one about Asia. I drank all night and most of the morning. I got a ride to Syracuse but lost my wallet and stuff. I almost got hit by a truck and bumped my head. I really couldn't remember anything."

"You're lying!" Asia screams, spraying a mouthful of beer across the room.

Mimi jumps in her seat.

"Where were you for all these weeks?" Wolfgang is still angrily eye-to-eye with Hershey.

"I was hanging out and drinking in different places until the accident. Then the nuns took me in. I live with them in Syracuse." She stops. "I really couldn't remember you until just now when I saw you."

Wolfgang stands and pushes the table away with the back of his legs. "Well it's too late." He looks down at Hershey. "We're over. No kissing and making up this time. I was only gone a week with Asia. When I came back I expected you to be here. Good thing I paid that farm boy down the street to take care of the kids, or they would have starved to death. I checked the answering machine, even sat around a few days waiting for you to call, but you disappeared for good."

He throws another cold look at an uncomfortable Mimi. "I guess no one thought to look for you in a convent."

Wolfgang walks over to Asia. They put their arms around each other. "I called Sydney last week. He drew up the papers for our divorce, and he's legally splitting our joint business ventures. I'm with Asia now. We may start performing together."

Hershey doesn't move, just looks sadly at Wolfgang.

"We had some fun, Mary Margaret...," Wolfgang begins again. "But you just can't stay away from the drugs and booze. That stuff will kill you some day, and I don't want to die. I want to have fun, spend some of that money we earned, which brings me to another point."

He disentangles himself from Asia and comes back to the table. He sits down again and softens his voice. "I also want to split all the royalties from our records, fifty-fifty. I take the motorcycles and you get the farm and the kids. Don't fight me on this, Mary Margaret."

Mimi sits upright when she hears that the kids will simply being given away. She remains silent.

Hershey's voice sounds beaten and sorrowful. "Okay, whatever you want. I'll sign the papers. Tell Sydney to arrange it all, and I'll sign."

"Good." Wolfgang stands and unfastens one of the diamonds in his navel. "I was afraid you might never show up, and I thought you might fight me on those royalties. Here." He hands the diamond to Hershey. "Something to remember me by. Sydney already faxed the paperwork to a law firm here in town, Cohen and Cohen. You passed their place on Main Street. You can stop and sign the papers on your way back. Asia and me will be out of here tomorrow. So you better come back and take care of the kids. There are six of them now."

He walks back to Asia who adds, "Smelly, crappy little things."

Hershey stands. "Okay, I'll sign the papers today. Is Sydney still my lawyer too?"

Wolfgang just shrugs his shoulders.

The conversation is over. Hershey and Mimi start for the door. Hershey turns back. "I just want to say...I mean...I'm sorry Dave. I never meant to hurt you. I really did love you."

Wolfgang says nothing but takes the beer out of Asia's hand and takes a big swallow.

Hershey and Mimi hurriedly descend the twelve steps, and Mimi is almost out of breath when she asks, "But where are the children, chère Hershey?"

"The kids?" Hershey corrects her. "Oh, I'll show you." She leads Mimi across the yard. They walk into the barn which is too hot from the closed windows and too smelly from manure that hasn't been cleaned in days.

"They're over here," Hershey leads on.

Mimi's eyes get larger, as they move to the back stalls. In a large mesh-enclosed stall are six young goats, two are black and white, two are beige, and two are black. They chew happily on hay and feed. Hershey checks their full water trays. "At least he's taking care of them, but this place needs a good cleaning."

Mimi is breathing into her blazer sleeve because of the pungent air in the barn. She's more than happy when they go back outside and head for the car. "But I don't understand. Where are zee children?" she asks.

"Kids is what they call baby goats," Hershey explains. "Wolfgang and I thought we wanted to retire and raise goats. It's a good thing we kept the major shares in the record company."

They get into their car, and Mimi hands a note to Hershey. "This was on zee wheel."

Hershey takes the small pink envelope and opens it. Inside is a card with a picture of her and Wolfgang in full costumes as *Talking Trash*. Hershey reads what Wolfgang has written. "Those were the good days. I loved you then, and I love you now, but we were just killing each other. Try and be happy, and I will too. With love, Your Wolfgang."

"Eez everything all right?" Mimi asks.

Hershey looks at the note again and puts it in her pocket. Then she answers, "Let's find the lawyer's office and then go home."

Mimi turns the car around and heads for the road.

CHAPTER 20

Mimi's driving skills are again tested as she descends the steep hill and follows Hershey's directions. They drive to Main Street and find the law offices of Cohen and Cohen. Mimi waits in the car while Hershey goes in to sign the legal papers. It only takes fifteen minutes, and Hershey returns clutching a manila envelope. "We can go now," is all she says. Mimi starts the engine and heads for Syracuse.

"I didn't get to see any of the Cohen Esquires," Hershey comments vacantly. "Their legal secretary was waiting for me. I just signed the papers and picked up my copies."

Hershey holds out the envelope. "Then she asked for my autograph for her brother. He used to buy all our records." Hershey stares out the side window. "I signed the autograph."

"You are feeling zee blues now, chère Hershey?" Mimi asks. "Eet eez a lot of emotion to happen to you, all at one time."

Hershey smiles at Mimi's "broken English" concern. "Yeah, this is a lot of emotion, but I'm okay. I'm more okay than I ever was as Mary Margaret O'Brien or Sky Volta."

She inhales deeply. "I feel good about myself for once. I haven't had a drink or a joint in weeks, and I don't miss' em. I don't even want' em. I just turned over several hundred-thousand dollars worth of interest in a record company for a deserted farm and some baby goats. And I think I may be happier with the goats."

Mimi smiles. "Eet eez a good attitude. You wheel be a good mother to baby goats. But..." Mimi hesitates. "What about zee divorce? Do you have zee broken heart?"

Hershey glances at Mimi. "I loved Wolfgang, or I think I did. You know when you're involved in show business, nothing is really real. You get pulled into the theater of everything. You're constantly performing; real life doesn't exist. I'm sure the drugs helped bend the reality too. Wolfgang and I were playing roles. We weren't real. We were performing most of the time even in our personal lives."

Hershey looks at the envelope. "My time with the Sisters is the closest thing to reality that I can remember. And I'm not sure how real your life is either."

Mimi steers back onto the Thruway. "So, now you have zee big decision."

"I thought I just made the big decision," Hershey responds. "What decision do I have now?"

Mimi laughs. "What name will you call yourself? Will you be Mary Margaret or Sky Volta, or will you be chère Hershey?"

I may just stay Hershey. I feel more like a Hershey than anyone else right now."

******

The end of the work-day traffic slows Mimi and Hershey's return trip. Jane's car is not in the driveway but neither of the women comment. No one wants to spread the fear that is building about the two missing Sisters.

They enter the back door and are engulfed in magnificent kitchen aromas. The smell of old fashioned pot roast, fresh baked bread, and homemade apple pie swirls around and pulls the two hungry women into the kitchen.

Samuel doesn't hear them enter. He stands at the stove vigorously stirring the gravy and humming in Hershey's rock and roll style. "What a Friend I Have in Jesus. Oh yeah!!"

Mimi and Hershey's attention is drawn to another person sitting in the kitchen. Her back is also to them, but she appears to be a young child. She is dressed in a denim skirt and a long- sleeved blouse with Indian designs on it. She also wears small garden gloves on her hands and an awkward looking rubber mask over her head.

Samuel turns from the stove and is momentarily startled. "Oh! You two scared me! I thought I locked that door. I never heard you come in."

The child runs to Samuel, who wraps his arms around the little girl. "Everything is fine. These are the two Sisters I told you about. You're safe."

Mimi and Hershey can see the front of the mask. It has a rather bizarre smiley face on it. Mimi calmly asks, "Who eez zee child?" Then she quizzically adds, "What eez wrong?"

"This is the package Jane told us to take care of." Samuel leads the girl by the hand back to the table. "Let's all sit down, and I'll explain everything. You did lock the door, didn't you?"

Hershey and Mimi now share Samuel's feeling of present danger. "It's locked," Hershey answers. "But why are the shades pulled down?"

"I think it's safer if no one sees us." Samuel coaxes the child to sit next to him.

Hershey and Mimi take their places across from Samuel and the child.

"This is Gabrielle," Samuel begins. "Charlie Lightfoot sent her in the back of a television repair truck. The driver was Charlie's cousin, and Charlie figured the IIA were still watching us. That's why Raymond brought her in here in a big cardboard box."

Samuel holds Gabrielle's gloved hand. "Gabrielle is a special child and is in grave danger. The IIA have captured Sean and Shakeeta and probably have Jane and Magdalene too. We may never see them again."

Mimi grabs Hershey's hand for support.

Samuel nervously pushes away his stray curl. "The IIA want to make Gabrielle disappear or maybe worse. Gabrielle isn't like us. She's from another place, not earth, but outer space. You know, up there somewhere in the heavens."

"A gift of God!" Mimi whispers. "Sister Culberth called them gifts of God."

"She is a gift of God," Samuel echoes the phrase. "But the IIA doesn't want anyone to know about her. We have to find a place to hide her, a safe place where no one, especially the IIA can find her."

He looks at Gabrielle and nods his head, as if he were reading some sign language. "Gabrielle wants me to tell you that she's wearing the mask and the gloves because she doesn't look like us. Her appearance may frighten us, so she wants to stay covered. She can't speak our language, but she can communicate with me through mind language."

He sees the confusion on Mimi and Hershey's faces. "I can read her thoughts, and she can read mine. It's really an amazing thing! It happened when I first looked at her. She made me feel calm like everything about me is now in harmony. I feel like I'm finally together, doing what I'm supposed to be doing, and that's helping people. I always wanted to help people. That's always been my purpose. Don't get me wrong, I don't have all the answers to my questions or problems, but they don't seem as important as being here right now, in this moment with Gabrielle and both of you."

Gabrielle pulls at Samuel's shirt sleeve. Samuel turns to her, nods, and then turns to Hershey. "Gabrielle says you know a place where she will be safe. You need to take us both there, and she'll take care of the kids."

"Not zee kids again!" Mimi exclaims.

"She must mean the farm." Hershey ventures a guess. "She

wants me to take you to the farm in Colden. It might be safe. It's pretty isolated, and no one knows I own it."

Mimi jumps in. "No one followed us today. I would have seen them on the big heel."

"Perfect." Samuel stands up like a drill sergeant. "Let's get some nourishment and have our evening prayers. Then Hershey, you can tell us how you plan to get Gabrielle to the farm with no one seeing us."

He returns to the cooking with Mimi as assistant chef. Hershey automatically sets the table working carefully around their guest who seems to enjoy the pre-dinner ballet.

"She doesn't eat meat or solid food," Samuel explains as he purees some potatoes and vegetables and pours the thick liquid into a glass. He puts in a straw and places the beverage in front of Gabrielle.

Mimi recites a short prayer, and they all eat in silence except for the gentle slurping of Gabrielle's straw as the liquid moves from the glass to the mouth-hole in the mask.

******

Hershey can't concentrate during evening prayers. She can't stop staring at Gabrielle, who sits next to the CD player and turns it on kinetically whenever Samuel gives her a signal.

How did Gabrielle know about the farm and the kids? And how will I get her there without the ILA finding out? Hershey struggles to push away her thoughts and finally closes her eyes. She tries to become one with the music.

Jane taught her to meditate with her senses not her mind. This will quiet all the clatter inside her head. She joins the music, and the candle flame, and the smell of the deodorant soap Samuel uses in his shower.

Hershey is in deep meditation. Her senses are keenly attached to the sound, the lights behind her closed eyes, the ringing of silence. She no longer smells Samuel's soap. She is floating away from Syracuse, away from the Sister's house, away from this room. She is floating outside of time and space on a sensory cloud, moving through some abstract continuum.

She bobs like a bubble in an aquarium. First up, then down, in a timeless slow motion. She moves through an indigo-colored space lit with twinkling stars, devoid of worry or concern, experiencing deep relaxation, deep joy....

"Hello." An Indian appears out of nowhere and floats in space with Hershey. "I'm Charlie Lightfoot. I sent you the child, so she will be safe. You need to call Marco."

With this last cryptic instruction, Charlie jets off into the indigo atmosphere and disappears. A small white feather floats to the ground. Hershey follows the feather and in the blink of an eye ends up flat on her back on the chapel floor.

Mimi, Samuel, and Smiley Face are all staring down at her.

"I almost have a plan," she says to the three worried faces. "I have to make a phone call."

******

Hershey is amazed at how easily Marco Carlotta's phone number comes back to her newly revised memory. Yesterday, she couldn't even remember any of her own names. The phone rings five times before Marco picks up.

"Yeah, whatda ya want?" a rough voice answers.

"Marco? This is...Sky Volta. I need your services." Hershey is evasive in case someone is listening in.

"Sky, Sky, you son-of-a-gun." The rough voice is lighter now. "I heard you was still around. Can ya talk?"

"No Marco it's too crowded. You know what I mean?" Hershey asks.

"Yeah, Yeah. Ya remember the old code?" Marco asks.

Hershey reaches back in her memory before answering. "I need a full twenty-one around midnight. Can you do it?"

"I haven't done a full twenty-one in a few years," Marco cackles back, obviously enjoying himself. "But you bet I can do it including the clothes. Midnight it is. Whatsa address?"

Hershey gives him the Sister's address and hangs up. She meets the others in the kitchen, and sits next to Mimi. "I need the money that Jane is keeping for me. I have a lot in the bank, but I don't have any identification. My lawyer can prove who I am, but we don't have time for that. I need some money to pay Marco."

"Who's Marco?" Mimi and Samuel ask at the same time.

"He's an old friend, a bodyguard I hired when I was performing. He's going to help us get Gabrielle to the farm, but I need a few hundred dollars for him."

She looks at Samuel. "Do you know where the money is?"

Samuel gets up, takes Gabrielle by the hand, and leads the way to Jane's office. Gabrielle sits on the short sofa while Samuel fishes around in the desk drawer for the key. He opens the bottom drawer and takes out the dented tackle box. He opens the box and inside is the roll of two hundred dollars that belongs to Hershey.

Samuel hands her the money. "This is yours." He moves papers and receipts and hunts around in the box until he finds a small brown envelope with several twenty dollar bills inside.

"This is the house money for the month." He hands the bills to Hershey. "I'm sure Jane would want us to use it to help Gabrielle."

Hershey takes the money and puts it all in her jeans pocket. Mimi sits next to Gabrielle, and Samuel joins them. All three look at Hershey.

"Let me explain the plan." Hershey motions the trio to bend closer. Then she turns on the CD player on top of the desk. *Music from the Mass of St. Rombold* plays in the background as she explains. "We should be careful, in case the office is bugged." She leans into the attentive listeners. "Here's what we're going to do. We all put on disguises and go to this punk nightclub called *Blood and Cabbages*. We have to look like we fit in and that includes Gabrielle."

Mimi and Samuel both look at Gabrielle, who sits between them. "And how will we do that?" Samuel asks incredulously.

"Marco is bringing the limo and the fat suit." Hershey feels a plan falling into place. "I haven't worn that suit in years, but I'm sure it'll work. Marco has lots of clothes that the two of you can wear." Hershey stops. "Wait here for a minute. I want to check something." She hurries into the living room and cautiously looks out the front window. The familiar green Lincoln is parked across the street. She hurries back into the office.

"They're out there all right." She catches her breath. "They must've started watching the house again after they captured Jane and Magdalene."

Her last comment causes another uncomfortable silence but before it can build to fear, Mimi speaks up. "What eez zee rest of zee plan please?"

"We make a lot of noise getting into the limo." Hershey gives more instructions. "You know, we want them to see us and to follow us. I used to do this all the time with Wolfgang when we wanted to ditch some clingy fans."

She searches in her jean's pockets. "You know, I think I used to smoke. I was just looking for my cigarettes. Guess I'm still remembering things. Anyway, when we get to the club, Gabrielle and I will change clothes with these actors that Marco hires. Then the two of us go out the back door to a rental car stashed there by Marco. Marco drives you two and the actors around in the limo for a few hours. By then, we should be at the farm."

Samuel looks at Gabrielle and nods his head as if in conversation. He turns back to Hershey. "Gabrielle wants me to go to the farm too."

"I'm not sure that's a good idea," Hershey responds.

"Why? There's not much for me to do here anymore. I want to take care of Gabrielle. She needs me, and I can speak for her."

"Mimi, tell Samuel that it isn't a good idea." Hershey looks at Mimi for help.

"I think eet eez a good idea, chère Hershey," Mimi replies. "I think Samuel wheel help you with zee child. I wheel stay here and pray for everyone. I wheel make zee IIA think zee house eez full with people until you all come back."

"Good, then it's settled." Samuel takes Gabrielle's hand and they stand. "We're going to take a nap until your friend Marco gets here. Gabrielle and I will be in my room if you need us."

Mimi also excuses herself and heads for the chapel, where she lights a candle and begins a litany of prayer petitions to all her favorite saints. She also prays for the absent Jane, Magdalene, and Culberth.

Hershey is alone in the dimly lit office, trying to put some meaning into the events swirling around her. She lost Wolfgang, but she's clean and sober. Lost her interest in a profitable record company, but is the proud owner of a goat farm. She may be a has-been punk rocker, but she has the opportunity to save the life of a...a...small child from a spaceship.

She closes her eyes and tries to picture Jane whose intelligence and ability to solve so many problems she truly misses at this moment. Hershey wonders what Jane would think about the plan.

"Jane would say this is a brave plan. She would tell me to trust what's inside me. Yes!" Hershey jumps to her feet. "Yes! This is going to work!"

She heads for her room to think, maybe to pray, while she waits for Marco. Maybe to try and push away her thoughts of kissing Samuel.

CHAPTER 21

Marco arrives promptly at midnight. The white stretch-limo takes up most of the driveway, and he blows the horn twice for added affect. He makes a big production out of getting bags and clothes from the back of the limo. By the time he reaches the door, he's carrying a box and suitcase and has clothes draped over both arms. Hershey greets him at the door and helps with a second trip to the limo for more.

Marco is a short Italian ex-boxer. His nose is slightly smashed and his balding head is accented by two cauliflower ears. He wears a formal-looking black suit and black tie, and the stub of a lit cigar dangles from the side of his mouth.

"I found da fat suit like ya asked." His voice is rough and gravelly.

"That's great!" Hershey holds up the one piece outfit and the blouse and attached pants roll down to the floor. "This will work just fine. What else do you have?"

Marco looks at the Sister, Brother, and masked girl lined up across from him in the kitchen. "Are dees da band?"

Not waiting for an answer, he fishes through a garment bag. "Dis is okay for da short one." He nods toward Mimi and holds up a zebra mini-dress with a green feather boa. "I got all kinds a shoes too."

He dives into a box and pulls out a purple polyester body stocking, "Dis'll fit da tall one. But I gotta go back to the limo for da make-up." He drops the body stocking on a chair and goes back outside.

Hershey hands the outfits to Mimi and Samuel. Both are more puzzled than shocked. "What will Gabrielle wear?" Samuel asks.

"She gets into the fat suit with me," Hershey explains. "Wolfgang and I did it tons of times."

Marco returns with a four-tiered make-up case and hands it to Hershey. Under his breath, he mumbles, "We gotta talk some business Sky."

Hershey turns to the others, "I think you should all go to my room and start changing. Take the make-up too."

They obediently leave, and Hershey and Marco sit at the table. "This is how it is, Marco. I lost my wallet, so I can't get into my money until I get a new set of ID's." She reaches into her pocket and pulls out the roll of two hundred dollars and the extra hundred from the house money. "I only have three hundred. This is all the cash I have. Can I owe you the rest?"

Marco reaches over and takes the money. He tucks it into the inside breast pocket of his jacket and moves his cigar from the left to the right side of his mouth. "I usually get five hundred for something like this. But for old times' sake and because the limo is free tonight, we can call it even." He offers Hershey his hand, which she enthusiastically shakes.

She pours Marco a cup of black coffee and takes the fat suit, matching jacket, and special shoes to her bedroom. She gives a little knock before she enters, but nothing, not even getting her memory back prepares her for the sight inside her room.

Mimi holds her grey polyester skirt in front of the zebra micro-mini. Her sleeveless top is open to the waist and held together with a white shoelace. Mimi's simple cotton bra is very visible through the lacing. Hershey decides not to mention the fact that this dress is usually worn without underwear. The bra seems a cool touch.

Hershey points to the dress and smiles. "That works."

"Eet eez very short," Mimi comments as she cautiously moves her grey skirt away.

"You only have to wear it for a few hours," Hershey bubbles supportively.

Samuel knocks quietly on the door. "I don't know if I can last very long in this outfit." He enters the room with Gabrielle.

The low-cut V-neck is the first thing to catch Hershey's eye. It accentuates Samuel's pectorals and smooth chest. The clingy purple polyester also accents his muscular arms and legs. It appears that every curve and contour of Samuel's body is highlighted by the body stocking.

Hershey's mouth involuntarily drops open. This is certainly a different picture of Samuel.

"I think it's too tight." Samuel brings Hershey back to earth. "I feel like you can see everything I own."

"No...No," Hershey stumbles but tries to reassure Samuel that he should wear the outfit. "No one will even notice you in this club. You'll fit right in. We don't have much time though, and we need to put on some make-up and get going."

Hershey's attention is suddenly drawn to the smiley mask. Hershey no longer has control over her own thoughts. Somewhere in her mind a message is transferred. *Try not to get worked up over Samuel's outfit. You might embarrass him.*

Hershey shakes the idea away and starts putting various make-up tubes, jars, and liners on the dresser. She shows the others how they will all wear the same make-up; bright white base, black lipstick, black eye shadow and snaky-looking, smeared green eyeliner.

Hershey and Samuel are putting on the last touches of green eyeliner when Mimi looks in the mirror at her finished product. "We all look like Wolfgang Merge!"

"That's the look we want." Hershey adds and the three of them burst into laughter which relieves some of their awkwardness.

Mimi kneels by the child. "I do this only for you, Gabrielle."

"She says, 'Thank you to all of us.' Samuel translates and puts his arm around Gabrielle.

Hershey unzips the fat suit and climbs into the legs. "Please, come over here?" Hershey gently motions to Gabrielle. "You need to stand in front of me, see. We both put our feet into the legs and then into the boots. I zip this up, and it looks like pants and a shirt."

Gabrielle follows Hershey's directions and climbs into the pants and boots. Hershey zips it up. "Can you breathe okay with that mask on? The shirt is supposed to be a breathable mesh. Are you okay?"

Samuel answers, "She can breathe fine. She likes being close to you."

Just as Samuel finishes translating, Hershey's body is enveloped in a warm, secure feeling of intense peacefulness and joy. She has a clear realization that like Gabrielle, she doesn't fit into this world. She is also an alien, living outside her true self. She can feel the frustration and loneliness of being an outsider but for this moment is removed from it. She is a self-appointed orphan just going along, desperately trying to find her way back home. She feels all these negative emotions, but they are outside her. She has moved out of her feelings and can look back at them objectively. Gabrielle has calmed the painful entities of Hershey's past life. They are solidified and captured in a large bell jar, so Hershey can separate from them and safely observe them. Hershey ponders her mistaken past and almost forgets what she's presently doing.

"Now what?" Samuel brings Hershey's alien melding to a more manageable state.

"Hand me that tie, please." Hershey finishes adjusting the shirt and tie before she adds the suit coat.

"The hard part for Gabrielle is that we have to walk together like we're one person. So, let's practice." Hershey starts walking around the room. Gabrielle feels almost weightless.

"This is no problem at all," Hershey tells the others. "But now we need to get into the limo and get going."

Hershey opens the bedroom door to leave, but Mimi stops her. "We must say a prayer, chère Hershey. That all wheel be well."

Hershey turns back, and the three white-faced punkers bow their heads and pray.

*****

Marco opens the limo door, and the punky threesome get into the luxury transport. They try to make enough noise for the whole neighborhood to hear them. Gabrielle still feels weightless as she sits on Hershey's lap. And Hershey continues to feel the warm calmness of her presence.

They are off to the Blood and Cabbages Club with Marco reporting every five minutes through the intercom. "I got da tail. He's still wid me. He ain't even try'n to hide."

They reach the nightclub, and Marco parks conspicuously in front. The limo takes up almost a block of parking spaces. He opens the door and the motley crew noisily emerges. He walks ahead and opens the door to the club and they enter a dimly lit hallway. They are immediately bombarded with deafening music. Mimi tries to say something, but her words evaporate into the loudness.

An extremely big bouncer in a sleeveless tee-shirt is first to greet them. He holds out his giant hand. "Ten dollars cover."

Hershey looks nervously at the other two. She never thought about a cover charge to get in. All the planning is about to fall apart when Mimi steps forward. She continues to tug on the hem of the zebra dress, trying unsuccessfully to lengthen it. She opens her large shoulder bag and takes out her grey, imitation-leather wallet with the praying hands clasp and pulls out some bills from a side compartment. She slowly counts out thirty dollars. "Eet eez from my birthday money," she tries to yell an explanation as she hands the money to the bouncer.

He stuffs the bills into his pocket and waves them into the dark club. All three stop at the end of the hallway and let their eyes adjust to the lights. The Club is a huge warehouse with exposed ceiling fixtures, pipes and wires. A long bar runs down the left side of the room, and tables and chairs are scattered around in no particular arrangement.

At the far end of the room, multi-colored flashing lights crisscross over a small thrust stage. Ceiling-high speakers also adorn each side. Four overweight men in torn jeans and undershirts are yelling incomprehensible words into standing microphones. A drummer sits behind them breaking numerous sticks, as he beats out a different rhythm than what they are yelling.

Hershey stops for a moment and lets her past life, her famous life, come flooding back to her. This used to be her home. Clubs like this one were all over the world, and they were where she felt like she belonged. She was a lot like Gabrielle. She wore a mask to hide her real self because she didn't fit in with her family, with her peers, or even with society, whatever that was. She always felt different, always felt like she was being chased by those who wanted her to fit into who they wanted her to be. Then she was chased by all those temptations, the drugs and the alcohol that made her feel like someone else, someone different but better.

The deafening music, the numbing booze and drugs, they just kept her from reaching out to her true being. Her past kept her from holding hands with her own soul. Being Sister Hershey and helping Gabrielle escape makes her feel truly integrated, more alive than she's ever felt.

She looks at the crowd of twenty-somethings dressed like Samuel and Mimi. They bob up and down in front of the stage and try to get caught in the flashing lights. They seem to be doing a dance which consists mostly of crashing into each other. From time to time, they scream in unison with the band, but the two words they scream are not really comprehensible.

Samuel thinks he hears, "Fun crew!"

Mimi hears, "Fudge too!"

Hershey knows it's time to find the hired actors. She motions the others to follow her toward the restroom which is opposite the bar. All three file into the two-stall Unisex restroom. The room's thick walls only block out some of the deafening noise.

"What happens now?" Samuel asks.

"We wait for the actors Marco hired to come in and change clothes with us. I'm not sure how long that will take. Marco said not to rush it. Spend enough time, so the guys following us won't get suspicious."

Two giggly girls, dressed in fringed blue leather bra tops and denim mini-skirts come into the lavatory. "Oh, really hot!" the first one points to Samuel's jumpsuit.

"Does it feel good getting poured into that?" The second one gushes as she goes into one of the stalls.

"Don't you just love the Hot Hemorrhoids?" The girl waiting asks Mimi. "Are they wild or what!" She practically jumps up and down.

The second girl comes running out and adjusts her skirt. Both look into the mirror at the same time. A lipstick comes out of the first girl's bra and she adds some dark blue to her existing black lipstick. Then she passes it to the other girl who adds more to hers. The first girl drops the lipstick back into her bra, and they wave good-bye as they leave.

"I don't love zee Hot Hemorrhoids." Mimi slides to the floor and sits down. She quickly puts her large purse in front of her exposed underwear.

Samuel comes closer to Hershey's fat suit and seems to be mentally talking to Gabrielle. He looks at Hershey. "Gabrielle says the discordant harmonies are making her sick."

"Is she going to throw up?" Hershey hurriedly asks. "I can let her out."

"No," Samuel reassures her. "She just wants us to sing something, so she can listen to us instead of that music."

Mimi thinks this is a good idea and with Samuel's help, she struggles back to her feet. They form a circle and start singing "Jesus Loves the Little Children." They move on to "Let There Be Peace on Earth," and work their way through three more pop hymns for the modern church. Just as they finish the mixed harmony of the last hymn, two other girls enter the room.

These two also wear the same white and black make-up, but they are at least five years older than the first set. Each one carries a tote bag with "Hot Hemorrhoids" on the front.

"Are you Sky Volta?" the first girl asks Samuel.

Samuel just makes a strange face and points to Hershey. "I'm Sky. I'm Sky Volta, Hershey says."

"Wow!" The girl comes closer to Hershey. "I mean. I thought you were dead or something. This is really cool. Can I get your autograph for my father?"

Hershey makes a painful face and nods a yes. The other girl steps closer. "And can I get one for my mother?"

"Sure, sure," Hershey says, disheartened but polite. "How did you know I was in here?"

"Marco sent us," the first one answers, handing Hershey two pieces of paper for autographs. "We're from the Star Glitz Agency.

We're here for the clothes switch."

Hershey signs the autographs and the clothes switch takes place. Samuel goes into stall one, and the first actress into stall two. They switch Samuel's jumpsuit for the actress's oversized stretch jeans and baggy, bare-midriff blouse.

They finish and Hershey takes the second actress's tote bag into stall two. She slides the fat suit under the stall to the second woman, who slides her leather mini-skirt and shear nylon blouse back to Hershey.

Hershey comes out of the stall leading Gabrielle, who is totally covered by a black hooded-cape. "What do you think?" she asks Samuel.

"I think you have nice legs but don't you think those boots have to go?" Samuel smiles at Hershey's exposed thighs and awkward-looking boots.

"My boots are my good luck charm, they stay." Hershey tries to stay focused. "What about Gabrielle?"

They all agree, including the two strangers, that Gabrielle is well hidden in the cape.

"We need to waste a little more time," the first actress instructs. "I think we should go have a drink and make sure we're seen."

Hershey throws a worried look at Mimi.

"I was donating my birthday money to zee Thrift Shop anyway, but I only have four dollars and eighty cents left."

"I'd love to buy the famous Sky Volta a drink," the second actress enthusiastically offers.

"And if that's Wolfgang Merge hiding in there," the other actress points to Gabrielle. "Well, I would love to buy him one."

"Great!" Hershey does not correct the misperception. "Let's all go get that drink."

They file to the bar and with unexpected fan worship and generosity share several four dollar colas. Another hour passes, and everyone agrees it's time to leave.

Mimi hugs Hershey and Samuel and puts her hand on Gabrielle's head. She whispers a special blessing.

The first actress hands Hershey a set of car keys. "It's the black Saturn in back." Then she leans in close to Hershey's ear and seductively says, "Thanks for the autograph. Sorry about Wolfgang losing his voice. Maybe he's upset about your split. I read about it in *Punk Scene Magazine.*"

The second actress leans in even closer to Samuel, her breast deliberately rubbing against his arm. In a low voice she says, "Marco knows my number if you ever get lonely or want someone to talk to."

She moves slowly away, again rubbing against Samuel's arm. The two actresses and Mimi make their way to the front door. Hershey gives them enough time to whistle for Marco and make a big show of getting into the limo. When they drive off, everyone hopes the IIA car will follow.

Hershey, Samuel and Gabrielle now head toward the dance floor. As they get closer to the stage, the music gets more deafening. Hershey sees the exit sign but getting to it involves moving through at least twenty bobbing and bashing dancers. Hershey is about to elbow through the first couple when Gabrielle lifts her hand and a clear path opens to the door.

The dancers who were blocking their way just seem to reposition themselves to allow this open walkway to the back door. Hershey has no time to think about how this was done. They just walk quickly to the door and exit. Hershey glances back and notices the empty path is again full of dancers.

The black Saturn is parked in a fire lane right next to the door. Hershey slides in behind the wheel while the others walk around the car and get in the passenger side. Hershey drives slowly out of the lot.

The ride to Colden is uneventful with Hershey checking her rear view mirror often. No one seems to be following. As a matter of fact, by the time they reach the small town, they are the only car on the road.

A sudden summer storm opens the heavens and results in teeming rain which makes the rural road dangerous and slippery. Visibility is difficult because of the force of the high winds. When they finally reach the base of the steep hill, Samuel turns to the back seat and has a silent conversation with Gabrielle. After an affirmative nod, he turns to Hershey. "Gabrielle wants you to pull over."

"Why?" Hershey doesn't take her eyes off the road. "This weather is brutal. I don't know if it's safe to pull off."

Samuel looks into the back seat again and repeats, "Please pull over. Gabrielle wants to drive the rest of the way."

Hershey throws Samuel an "Are you crazy" look. But Samuel quietly adds, "I think you should let her drive."

Hershey gives in and is about to run out into the rain to switch places with Gabrielle when Samuel says, "Gabrielle says you can stay where you are. Please keep your hands off the wheel, put your car in neutral, feet off the gas and brake."

Hershey reluctantly obeys, and the car is smoothly and carefully guided up the hill. It feels like the car is floating above the road rather than traveling on it. At the top of the hill, the rain turns to a drizzle and the car lands and stops. They all take a moment to watch the early morning sun come up over the tops of the distant trees. The beauty of the moment lingers until Hershey finally says, "The farm is just down this road."

Before she can put her hands back on the wheel, the car is off again. The automatic pilot guides the car into the farm driveway. Hershey notices all the house lights are off except for the one above the front door. The car pulls next to the house, parks, and shuts off. The motorcycles and all-terrain vehicle are gone.

The rain stops completely as they walk up the twelve steps to the door. Hershey remembers she doesn't have a key and hopes Wolfgang will let her in. She knocks on the door but no one answers. She knocks again and still there is no answer. She tries the handle and the door opens.

They enter and make their way to the still messy living room. A folded note is taped to the silent television screen. Hershey unfolds the note.

It reads: "Dear Sky, the place is all yours now. See you in the movies. Your past love, Wolfgang Merge."

A dull pain touches Hershey's heart as she thinks of Wolfgang. Another twinge of pain hits her when she thinks of Jane who would understand all of this. Jane would know what to say to make it easier. Hershey refolds the letter, tucks it in the top of her boot and turns back to Samuel and Gabrielle. "Everyone is gone and the farm is safe. This is our home for now."

CHAPTER 22

A loud knock rouses the Yellow Man crouched in his guard position. He unlocks the door and Whittington strides confidently across the room to Jane and Magdalene's cage.

"Two days and nights in a dog kennel and neither of you wants to change your story. We want that alien, and we know you have information that can help us." He adds smugly, "You two aren't getting bored in there are you?"

Jane controls her tongue which is not easy since she's definitely irritable from her confinement. She knows this young man needs some manners. "Sisters don't really get bored, but you probably..." She pauses for affect. "You probably don't remember much about those Sisters who taught you, cared for you, and prayed for you."

She starts getting too involved. He's the latest cause. He's the latest lost sheep that needs to be brought back home. How much of her life has been spent finding and saving lost sheep? Sheep members of her family, sheep from her community, sheep that intentionally hurt her and then needed her to help them find their way back home. "Sister Magdalene and I were just discussing *The Book of Ruth*. We lost all track of time. You know these Biblical discussions can go on for days or even weeks."

Whittington steps away from the cage. "How long can those discussions go on with only one person? Huh? How would you like to be in separate cages or maybe separate buildings or separate states? How would you like that?"

Jane pushes her fear away. "We know we may be persecuted, and we know we're never alone. Maybe you forgot your teachings Edward, but Sister Magdalene and I still know how to pray. We don't need to be together to pray as one."

Whittington grimaces and starts for the door. Before opening it, he turns back. "We'll see how well you pray as one, when she..." He points to Magdalene. "Gets flown out of here tonight, and you stay behind."

He slams the door, and Yellow Man grins as he takes his crouching position again.

Magdalene is visible shaken. Her face looks like white semi-gloss paint on a new wall. Her hands are shaking, and she bites her lower lip so hard, Jane fears it will bleed. They sit next to each other, arms around each other.

"I'm afraid," Magdalene whispers. "I know I can be unyielding sometimes, I know I bear the sin of self-righteousness, but acting strong and acting like I'm in control makes me feel less afraid. Right now, I'm not in control and I'm afraid. I'm more afraid for you than for me. I don't care where they relocate me. I'm strong and healthy, and I can work for my meals. But I'm afraid to leave you alone again Jane. I promised myself I would never let you be locked up again, but now I don't think I can prevent that from happening."

Jane smiles at her old friend and hugs her closer. "That's one of the nicest things anyone has ever said to me Maggie." She rocks them slightly back and forth. "But we aren't separated yet. I have faith that something will happen before that plane arrives to take you away. We need to have faith."

******

Minutes, then hours seem to drag by. Jane can't tell if it's day or night since their prison is in a windowless room. She looks at her watch and sees it's nine o'clock at night.

Magdalene, as if reading Jane's thoughts, gets up from the stiff cot. She sits next to Jane. "I've prayed very hard especially to St. George, and I've beseeched my Grandmother Myrtle. Something miraculous will save us."

Jane smiles at Magdalene's simple, strong faith. Suddenly, rather miraculously, a whooshing sound like a giant fly swatter being swung through the air sends the far wall of the room crashing into fist-sized bits of concrete. Yellow Man is hit on the head by a flying mini-slab and crumbles unconscious in his crouching spot.

Jane and Magdalene huddle together turning their faces away from the exploding wall. Scattering debris flies around them, and Jane looks back just in time to see the entrance of a huge, milky-colored transparent bird-like creature.

He walks through the hole into the room. The creature is nearly twelve feet tall. His body is almost human-like but with no noticeable gender, like a toy doll. His arms are attached to white feathered wings with a span that almost reaches both sides of the room. His hands and feet are identical with two protrusions for fingers on each hand and identical protrusions for each foot.

As unusual as this bird creature is, Jane finds herself drawn instantly to its head which looks like a diaphanous holograph. Not quite real but more like a movable still life. His facial features play like a newsreel of various human heads morphing from one appearance to another, first female then male then back again. He has no eyes, mouth, or solid features. Everything about him seems to be liquid and changes every second.

Magdalene opens her eyes and looks up at the new visitor. "IT'S AN ANGEL!" She's almost breathless as she runs to the bars of the cage, trying to get closer to the creature. "Are you St. George or

Grandmother Myrt?"

Jane doesn't try to stop Magdalene; she just sits back on the cot and stares at the huge quasi-projection that fills the room. She begins to worry about what will happen next when a warm feeling of absolute calm seems to radiate from the glowing transparent bird. This feeling of wellness washes over Jane and Magdalene and fills their beings. They immediately relax and bask in the afterglow of peace emanating from the bird creature.

"Excuse me!" A cavernous voice comes from the center of the creature, but its mouth still moves differently with each morphed head. "I'm experiencing technical difficulty; please do not adjust your set." The bellowing voice continues.

Magdalene leans in to Jane. "This is wonderful!" She spontaneously grabs Jane's hand. "We must thank God for sending us an angel."

Jane isn't quite sure how to respond to this new development in their situation or how to respond to Magdalene. She knows that in the throes of adversity, hope is essential, so she says softly and with little enthusiasm, "Thank you, God."

"Thank you! Thank you! Thank you!" Magdalene jumps up screaming, throwing her arms in the air. Finally, she pushes against the bars of the cage and yells to the creature, "I know you are one of God's angels. You've come to deliver us from evil. Can you tell us your name? Is your name George or Myrtle?"

The angel-creature takes a step toward the cage and lowers its wings. In a monotonous, fog-horn voice, it blares, "Please step to the rear and the door will open."

Magdalene steps back by Jane, and the cage door blows off into the room. The two women rush out of the cage with Magdalene falling to her knees in supplication and prayer.

Jane feels she should say something but first assesses the

situation. *Perhaps this is a dream.* "Thank you." She asserts a stiff proper tone then hesitates. "Are you an angel?"

The voice from the creature's center booms out his reply. "I have studied you Earth creatures. My greatest resource is your television, your everyday encyclopedia of culture and social mores. I tried to get here sooner, but all that space trash slowed me down. I actually collided with some floating garbage labeled, 'Station.'"

He stops momentarily and raises his wings to waist height. In a loud reverberating voice he adds, "Someone doesn't recycle."

His voice is so loud and vibrating that this last statement bounces off the wall behind Jane causing her to cover her ears. Magdalene also covers her ears but quickly recovers and demands, "Well, are you an angel?"

The creature puts his wings down again and booms, "I'm not a pop-up toaster strudel. You can be an angel or smile you're on a *Candid Camera.*"

A strange high-pitched laugh fills the room. This is followed by, "Sorry, just kidding." The creature gets serious. "I hope you will think of me mostly as a father."

Magdalene now has her doubts. "Do you mean you're some kind of priest? Well, I for one am not prepared to call a giant angel, 'Father'."

"Not that kind of father," the creature blasts back. "I have a daughter. Her picture's not on milk cartons, but she's lost. I came to you for help in finding her."

"Do we look like the lost and found?" Magdalene huffs sarcastically. She looks at Jane. "I told you those last two hamburgers were spoiled, and see, I'm hallucinating from food poisoning."

Jane puts a reassuring hand on Magdalene's shoulder. "You're not hallucinating. This is an unusual sort of angel." She hopes Magdalene will be more comfortable with less knowledge. "I think he will help us get out of here."

She turns to the creature. "You're here to save Gabrielle. Isn't that right?"

"Yes, my network has been in a dead zone," the creature bellows. "I am Luminescence, but you can call me Lou, and the one you call Gabrielle is my daughter, Amoria. Her transport was lost in a black hole, and she ended up here with the largest selection of sofas stocked for delivery. I thought I knew exactly where she was but due to technical difficulty my cable went out."

Magdalene is thoroughly confused. "You don't talk like an angel."

Jane sees an opportunity and takes it. "Of course he's an angel." She tries to add more assurance to her voice. "I think Luminescence translates to George. Don't you see, Magdalene, our prayers are answered."

Magdalene looks skeptically at Jane then at the creature. But before she can say anything, the creature blares. "Where is my daughter?"

"We don't know for sure," Jane answers. "But we do know how to track her down. We think our friends have her hidden. We know she must still be safe or the IIA would have stopped questioning us."

"These men are evil, like tough clogs in your sink drain," the creature responds. "I will kill them."

"No! No!" Jane is appalled at the thought. "You can't just kill people. We need to change them, to make them think differently. We need to turn Whittington back to the nice young man I think he once was."

"ARE YOU CRAZY, JANE!" Magdalene yells. "Whittington kept us in a cage and relocated my nephew and his wife, and who knows how many others. He is at this moment getting a plane to separate us, so he can break us into telling him what happened to

Gabrielle. He's not a nice young man."

"Every person has value," Jane reminds Magdalene. "And with your help, Lou or Angel George..." she winks at the creature. "I think we can turn Whittington around and maybe get the IIA to release all those relocated people. Will you help?"

"I will do what needs to be done to prevent cavities from forming and to get my daughter home," the creature trumpets.

******

"No one even knows this airfield exists." Whittington puts his feet up on the desk again as he talks into the phone. "What are you so worried about? The President shut down the IIA before. The closing lasts about a day. They fire a few executives, and we're back in business. Oh yeah, this time is different. I heard that the last time. Look, can you fly her to the relocation camp or not? What's wrong with you? No. No one can hear this conversation. For God's sake, no one can hear anything in this place. A bomb could fall down the hall, and I wouldn't know it until I walked back there. Okay. I said, okay. You're here at eleven, or you're not coming. That's fine, yeah, goodbye."

He takes his feet off the desk and puts the cell phone back into his jacket pocket. He picks up a magazine, leans back in his chair and starts leafing through the pages.

Whittington's quiet moment is, however, suddenly broken by the crashing sound of the concrete wall behind him. It crumbles and flies all over the room. He jumps to his feet and draws his gun from his shoulder holster. His arms move instinctively to protect his head and face.

Angel George slowly emerges from the huge hole in the wall, legs and feet first and then feathered arms, and morphing hologram head. Whittington carefully and deliberately aims his gun. He tries to steady it with both hands. "I'm an agent of the IIA!"

Luminescence straightens his body to full height and bellows. "And what will that weapon do, kill bad breath germs and prevent plaque from forming?"

"Don't come any closer," Whittington orders in a shaky voice. His hands tremble and the gun noticeably bobs up and down.

Luminescence then recites his given lines in his best basso voice. "I am an angel. I've come to save your soul, if I can, and the price is right."

"You're not an angel!" Whittington yells back. "You're here to invade earth and destroy all humans."

"How silly you are," Luminescence answers. "Perhaps you have a beating headache pain."

"I don't have a headache." Whittington keeps his aim on the angel. "You'll have to kill me to go any further. I'm trained to die in the line of duty."

"Trained to die," Angel George repeats Whittington's words. "Well, that might put new highlights in your hair. We need to change people, to make them see things differently."

With this last comment, Luminescence brings his wings up and Whittington is bathed in a bright white light. He feels his whole being covered in calm, peace, and love. He hasn't felt this way since he was a child. He puts the gun down and falls limply to his knees. "Are you really an angel?" He asks in a soft voice.

"Well...ah..." Luminescence hesitates but bellows on, "I am Angel George. You and the IIA did some bad things. You need to change, right now or no amount of scrubbing can help you. A scummy coating has built up on you. Do you understand me, Edward?"

Still on his knees, Whittington feels the peaceful light beginning to ebb away. He quietly says, "Yes, I know what you're talking about, but I can change. I can go to Washington and tell the President what's really going on. He wants to know the truth. He wants to close the IIA for good. I can tell him about the relocation centers."

"That would be good, Edward," Luminescence resonates back. "And what about the other things the IIA did? Will you tell the President about those?"

"I don't know for sure about the experiments." Whittington's voice is cracking and his head is bowed. "I heard stories from the others, but I never saw the labs or the graves."

He looks up at the strange angel. "I can tell him what I heard. I was supposed to deliver the alien to another agent. I can give them his name and the location. Oh Angel George will I be forgiven? I'm sorry for everything I've done. I just wanted to make a lot of money. You know, earn enough to ask Amy to marry me, and settle down in a very expensive townhouse outside of Chicago. I didn't mean to hurt anyone. This was a government job. My mother wanted me to work for the government."

Lou taps his two-toed foot. "Stop blaming everyone else and take some responsibility. Rust doesn't happen overnight. You're getting a second chance, and you can thank those two Sisters. And you better do what you promised; tell the president, shut down the IIA and the labs, free the prisoners...or blemishes will keep returning."

Luminescence suddenly turns into a bright ray of multi-colored light and shoots out the small open window above the desk.

Whittington gets up and runs to the window straining to see the disappearing light. He yells after the vision, "I will! I promise! I'm a new man. I'm not soap scum anymore!"

He hurries down the long hallway to where the Sisters are caged. He sees the huge hole in the wall. Magdalene and Jane are huddled around a cot nursing and ministering to the Yellow Man, who is lying flat on his back.

Jane looks up at Whittington and says flatly, "He's going to need medical attention. There's a nasty bump on his head."

"He was here wasn't he?" Whittington nervously asks. "The angel was here, wasn't he?"

"Oh yes," Magdalene answers. "Angel George was here. He told us you would take us home. Is that true?"

"Yes! Yes! Everything he said is true!" Whittington takes the cell phone out of his pocket and punches in a number. "I want you to get an ambulance and a plane here right away. I need two people flown back to Syracuse tonight."

He lowers the phone and pleads with the Sisters. "Will you forgive me for what I did to you? I'm really sorry."

"Of course you're forgiven." Jane says nudging Magdalene.

"I'll consider forgiving you when my nephew and niece are safe, and when I'm back in my own home, in my own room. Then I'll think about forgiving you." Magdalene says curtly.

CHAPTER 23

Jane and Magdalene are silent during their ride from the Syracuse Airport to their home. Magdalene glares at the oversized head of their burly ex-captor, Gorilla Man. He maneuvers the dark green Lincoln into their driveway and politely opens the door for Jane. She slides out and walks to the house. Magdalene waits for the driver to walk around and open her door.

Gorilla Man gives her a wide capped-teeth grin. "No hard feelin's, I hope."

Magdalene pulls her weary body into perfect posture. "Of course there are hard feelings. Look at me! I was kept in a cage. I haven't bathed in days. I haven't even brushed my teeth. I...I have hard feelings toward you!"

The large grin slowly leaves the gorilla's face. His eyebrows wrinkle in remorse. "I'm sure sorry lady. I was just doin' my job. I tried not ta hurt ya."

"You're sorry, you were just doing your job," Magdalene repeats his words, as she builds her assault. "Let me tell you something. I am not 'Lady'. I'm Sister Magdalene, and I have taught boys like you, and I knew what would happen to you. You are ill-mannered, disrespectful, bad boys."

She catches herself and realizes this is a grown man she is talking to. "You should be ashamed of yourself."

Gorilla Man diverts his eyes to the ground. "I was fired. They're closin' down the company." He reaches into his back pocket and takes a business card out of his wallet. He still doesn't make eye contact but hands it to Magdalene. "I'm goin' into business for myself. If ya ever need protection just call or fax. I'll always give ya a discount."

Magdalene snaps the card out of his hand and stomps to the back door where Jane is ringing the bell. Gorilla Man backs out of the driveway.

On the fourth ring, Mimi finally answers the door. "Mere Maria!" She throws open the door and tries to hug both women at once. She plants emotional kisses on both their cheeks. "Ma amie Jane, Magdalene, you are alive! You are okay!"

"We are fine." Jane tries to keep her composure but feels a release of emotions creeping into her voice. "We are glad to be home too." Jane feels tears trickling down her face.

Magdalene sees the tears. "Oh Jane, now you've done it." She also begins to cry, sobbing alternately on Jane's shoulder then on Mimi's.

Jane tries to move everyone inside the house which proves to be difficult since Mimi also starts crying. Once the clinging trio is in the kitchen, Jane collects herself and hands everyone tissues. This seems to soothe some of the heightened feelings.

Mimi puts on the kettle and offers her Sisters some fresh-baked banana surprise muffins. The surprise is they aren't really muffins.

Magdalene's exhaustion gets the better of her, and she unexpectedly announces, "I'm even too tired for tea. I just want a long bath and my own bed."

Jane encourages Magdalene to fulfill her momentary wishes. She remains in the kitchen to catch up on what has happened. Jane takes a small sip of the steaming tea and puts the warm cup back on the table. "Did Charlie Lightfoot deliver the package here?" she asks.

Mimi looks from side to side and moves closer to Jane before answering. "He has zee friend deliver her in a box. Then we all follow zee plan of Hershey." Mimi lowers her voice and whispers, "They are all gone for two days. I think they are safe."

Jane takes another sip of tea and before her curiosity can get the best of her asks, "What was Hershey's plan?"

Mimi, still barely audible, goes into a lengthy discussion of Hershey and her trip to the farm, Marco and his stretch limo, dressing in 'revealing' clothing and a fat suit so they fit into the club. Also in her explanation is how she spent the rest of that evening as a decoy, traveling to four more Hot Spots with two young actresses who wanted to know if Mimi ever slept with Wolfgang Merge.

Jane stops Mimi at this point and out of personal interest asks, "What did you tell them?"

"I try to fit in," Mimi explains. "And I have zee free glass of red wine at Club Hot. So I say, 'Yes. Yes, we sleep together. We eat together and do everything together.'"

Mimi pauses and sips more tea before continuing. "They say, 'How is he?' I am not understanding ma amie Jane. I am getting a pain in zee head from red wine and zee bad music. So I say, 'He eez good, but he does not like kids.' They ask no more questions after that."

Jane pulls herself back to the business at hand. "Can you take me to the farm?"

"Yes," Mimi answers. "I know how to get there but eez eet safe to go?"

"We must go tonight," Jane explains. "Gabrielle's father is looking for her, and I promised we would help him find her. I can get in touch with him at six o'clock, and then we must leave. That gives me a little time to clean up and rest."

Mimi gets up and carefully looks out the kitchen window. She can see the driveway and part of the street. "What about zee IIA? Will they not follow us and take Gabrielle?"

"The President of the United States is investigating the IIA," Jane explains. "Agent Whittington should be arriving in Washington any minute now to tell about the relocation centers and the other dirty business involving the IIA."

"Edward...Agent Whittington told me most of the agents have been notified that they no longer have jobs. Some were questioned by the FBI and charges may be brought against them. Magdalene and I may both have the opportunity to press charges but that isn't my present concern. We need to reunite Gabrielle and her father."

She pauses and silence returns to the house, but only for a moment. A piercing scream cuts through the stillness. "Jane! Jane! Help me! Help me!" Magdalene is crying out from the hallway.

Jane and Mimi race from the kitchen to her aid. They run into the hallway and find Magdalene standing outside of Hershey's room, her back against the wall.

Magdalene is naked. She unsuccessfully tries to drape a bathtowel around herself. "I forgot my nightgown." She anxiously tries to explain. "I was just sneaking across the hall to my room, and Hershey's door was slightly opened. I looked in. There's a body leaning against the window. It's terrible! Look, Jane, look!"

Mimi can't take her eyes off Magdalene's unaccustomly exposed body. She awkwardly tries to explain. "No Magdalene. This eez not a body." She goes into the bedroom and returns carrying a life-sized stuffed doll. "Eet eez zee scarebird," Mimi continues. "I make two of them and move them from room to room, so zee IIA does not miss Hershey and Samuel."

"Scarebird?" Jane asks.

"She means scarecrow." Magdalene is terribly annoyed. "The least you could have done was tell us you had these things lying around the house." Magdalene twirls around and stomps off to her room, leaving Jane and Mimi and the "scarebird" in the quiet hallway.

Mimi looks at Jane and whispers, "No tattoo."

They both start to giggle.

******

At exactly six o'clock, Jane goes into the living room and turns on the television. The channel selector is moved to their clearest station. As the news anchor begins the lead stories, Jane puts her hands on the screen and calls out. "Luminescence...Lou...if you can hear me, we know where your daughter is and we will take you to her. Please don't come into the house. We can't afford the repairs. If you can hear me just follow the old grey Chevy."

Jane takes her hands off the screen and clicks off the television. She turns around and sees Mimi and Magdalene staring at her. Mimi asks, "Who eez Luminescence?"

Magdalene answers for Jane. "He says he's an angel and his name is George."

"You have zee Angel Georges in your television?" Mimi asks.

"He's not really in the television," Jane attempts a better explanation. "But he told me that was a good way to get in touch with him."

"Zee angel wheel come to zee farm?" Mimi tries again.

"The angel is really Gabrielle's father," Jane tries again too.

"But of course, Gabrielle and Luminescence." Mimi tries to make the connection but can't quite do it. "We must go now. Zee night eez dark and zee big heel eez difficult for an old car."

******

Magdalene sits in the back seat and says nothing. She does emit a slight gasp when Mimi nonchalantly conveys the fact that Samuel quit his job and is leaving the Community.

Jane politely interrupts Mimi's ongoing saga. "Did Samuel say why he quit the hospital?"

Mimi stops her story to explain. "He say zee hospital eez political and do not care for poor men on zee street."

Magdalene forces herself to be calm. "And what was his reason for leaving the Community?"

"He never truly explains this." Mimi answers. "We get off zee thought train and start to understand Jane's message about zee package."

"Off the track Mimi." Magdalene corrects her. "You got off the track not the train."

The car falls back into awkward silence again until Mimi slowly brings the already creaking Chevy to a stop. "This eez zee big heel." She points into the ascending darkness ahead.

"It looks very steep." Jane cranes her head to see how far up it goes.

"Eet eez a pisser." Mimi shifts the car into second gear.

"What did you say?" Magdalene acerbically asks. "Did you say 'pisser'? Where did you learn such a word?"

Mimi starts inching the car up the hill. "I learn from zee girls in zee limo. They use many new words for me."

Magdalene sits back and dryly commands, "Don't ever say 'pisser' again, please. And you may want to test some of those other words with me before you use them in everyday conversation."

The old car creaks and vibrates like a weightlifter trying to break a new record. It takes almost five minutes to travel only a hundred feet. A putrid burning rubber smell starts to seep into the interior of the car.

"I think we may be burning out the engine," Jane cautions.

"Is it the brakes?" Magdalene asks in a nervous tone. "Do you have your brakes on?"

Mimi doesn't answer. Her hand grips the shift. She can feel the engine slipping, so she steers the car over to the grassy shoulder of the road. "I do not think we make zee heel." She puts the car into first and keeps her foot on the brake. "I think we must go back."

Almost Biblically, a sudden flash of white light glows in the middle of the road.

"Here he comes," Magdalene says under her breath.

The white light grows into the giant amorphous figure of Luminescence. Magdalene whispers to Mimi. "Do you think he really looks like an angel?"

"Mère Marie!" Mimi crosses herself. "Eet eez *really* an angel!"

Jane hastily gets out of the car and walks to Luminescence. He booms at her, "So after twenty washings where is my daughter?"

"The farm is at the top of this hill," Jane tries to explain. "Our car can't make it up, so we may have to walk."

"No need to walk," Luminescence fog horns again. "You're in good hands. Please return to your seat and fasten your seat belts. We will take off momentarily."

Jane does not question what is about to happen. She hurries back to the car and tells everyone to buckle up.

Luminescence spreads his wings across the road in front of the car. It slowly lifts straight up off the ground and moves languidly to the top of the hill, where it is then gently lowered back onto the road. During the tension of the initial take-off, the three passengers are bathed in a warm feeling of calm and contentment. Only when they are on the ground again does this intense sense of well-being gradually leave them.

"Zee angel eez much better than tranquilizers," Mimi comments as she starts down the road.

******

"I thought you were resting?" Hershey walks over to Samuel who kneels by the fireplace poking the dying flames.

"I did lay down with Gabrielle for a few minutes." He looks back at the dying embers. "You know what she said to me? It choked me up." Samuel turns and sits cross-legged on the floor.

Hershey sits next to him. "What did she say?"

"Gabrielle said she hopes her father will find her." Samuel's faltering voice reveals the deep emotion he is feeling. "Gabrielle wants to go home."

"Well, maybe she will." Hershey tries to stay hopeful.

"How?" Samuel asks rhetorically. "How can we ever get her home?"

They sit silently thinking. "Jane will know how to get her home," Hershey says.

Sadness fills Samuel's voice as he answers, "We can't even get Jane home."

Hershey takes Samuel's hand and looks into his eyes. She is insistent but also reassuring. "Jane's safe. She'll be okay and Magdalene too. I have enough faith to believe that everything will work out."

A familiar jolt of electricity passes between them. Samuel stares at Hershey as he has several times before. They're two magnets trying to fight their natural pull toward each other, caught in a timeless energy field, eye to eye, feeling to feeling, and finally lips to lips. They kiss deeply with the subtle passion of knowing each other for a long time, maybe in another life, maybe on another planet.

Samuel suddenly jerks away. "I'm sorry." He gets up and puts several feet of space between Hershey and himself. Hershey gets up to face him.

He turns away and crosses his arms, wrapping them tightly around his body. "I shouldn't have let that happen. I'm really sorry, Hershey."

Hershey walks in front of him forcing him to look at her. "I'm not sorry. Why are you so upset? What happened that was so bad?"

Samuel looks at her. This time the magnetic force is hidden behind his sadness. "It wasn't fair to you, Hershey." He says. "I've been questioning so many things lately; my calling, even my vows which I take as seriously as my Army oath."

He walks back to the fireplace and stares into the ashes. Hershey follows, and he looks at her. "Before you came to live with us, I was pretty sure I wanted to be a priest or at least an ordained Brother."

He looks back at the fire. "Now I'm about to make another big change. My life with the Sisters was safe. It helped me escape life after the war; life after my fiancé got tired of waiting and fell out of love with me. I've been trying to escape from the world for a long time. I think leaving the safety and anonymity of the convent life will be the toughest decision I ever make."

He walks to the window overlooking the clover-carpeted pasture. Hershey stays by the fireplace. She can't sort out what is happening. Samuel turns back. "That decision got easier when all the problems started at the hospital and when you came to live with us."

He shakes his head. "I never met anyone who looked like you or acted like you. You were/are so full of life and excited about all the little things I took for granted. I was envious of Mimi because she spent all that time with you. I kept feeling my heart pound a little faster whenever you came close to me. At first, I couldn't understand all these feelings. I thought they were gone, maybe killed in the war. But I felt something whenever you were around. You made me feel energized about things even the way you sing. I should have guessed you were a singer. We all should have figured that out."

He stares out the window at the clover. "I really tried to fight those feelings," he says softly to the outdoors. "I prayed and meditated. I even discussed some of it with the chaplain at the hospital."

He turns back to Hershey. "He told me, I was falling in love and that was a very human thing to do. The only problem would be reconciling my love for another human being with my holy orders. 'They don't always mix' were his exact words."

His voice grows hushed. "I planned to run as far away from you as I possibly could. I thought you'd stay at the convent, and I would leave. You know, I'd go somewhere for awhile and try to figure out what all this human love really means. Then Gabrielle came into the picture."

He moves closer to Hershey. "You can't imagine what being with her for these few days has done to my thinking and my feelings."

"I know you two have a really special bond." Hershey finally breaks her silence.

"Gabrielle has helped calm me from the world and from myself," Samuel explains. "She's helped me see all the love and caring I thought was missing in myself and in others around me. Gabrielle has confirmed my old belief that all love is good. That love is the state we should try to be in constantly. She put me back in touch with others and with God."

Samuel stops talking. Hershey takes his hand and moves closer. Their eyes still have a tunnel vision for only one other person in the whole universe. Hershey leans into their private energy field. Their mouths are slightly open for a second kiss. They are separated by only a breath when the doorbell rings. Both jump at the same time. Hershey drops Samuel's hand and stares at the front door. "Who the hell can that be?" She asks nervously.

"Maybe the IIA," Samuel whispers as he runs for the bedroom. "Try to stall them. I'll get Gabrielle and hide her in the barn."

He stops and looks back at Hershey. "They can't find her."

Hershey waits for Samuel to reach the back bedroom, and then she moves to answer the persistent bell. Her brain can't concoct a plan in such short notice, but she does remember how to pray. She sends a plaintive, "Please help me" to anyone celestial who may be listening. Prepared for any fate, she cautiously opens the door.

Mimi smiles broadly as she stands in front of Jane and Magdalene. "All eez well, chère Hershey."

Hershey can't speak. She just grabs Mimi and hugs her, then grabs Jane and the resistant Magdalene and wraps her arms around them. "I can't believe this! Jane! Oh Jane! And Magdalene! You're both safe!" She stops suddenly. "But should you be here? Were you followed?"

"It is a miracle." Magdalene stoically pushes Hershey's embrace away.

Jane hugs back but quickly asks, "Where's Gabrielle? We have her father with us. He wants to take her home."

Hershey looks out the door. "Where is her father?"

"He disappeared again." Magdalene offers. "He seems to do that."

"He eez an angel," Mimi adds excitedly.

Hershey leads them all into the living room. Mimi looks around. "Oh, you have cleaned up zee sheet."

"Sheet?" Magdalene repeats. Then she mentally translates. "I asked you not to use those words Mimi."

Hershey covers a grin with her hand and motions for them to follow her down the back hall. She opens the bedroom door expecting to find Samuel and a sleeping Gabrielle. Instead, she just finds Samuel huddled in a ball under the covers.

"Sam?" Hershey cries out, confused that Gabrielle is not there and surprised at her familiarity with Samuel's name.

Samuel sees the sisters and bounces off the bed. He starts another round of hugs. "This is wonderful! Jane, Magdalene, you're both safe! Thank God! Thank you, God!"

Jane, still in Samuel's embrace quickly asks, "Where is Gabrielle?"

"I don't know," Samuel answers. "I came to get her, and she was gone. I looked in the other bedrooms, but she's not there either. When I heard voices heading this way, I decided to get under the covers and hope it would distract you."

"She's probably in the barn," Hershey offers as she leads them to the back door. "She loves those baby goats. It's funny really. I never wanted the goats, but their mother was killed in a barn fire, and kids can't live without their mother, not without help. I don't think I knew what I wanted, but Wolfgang thought it would be cool to make goat-milk fudge. Then I disappeared. I don't think they ever had any real love until Gabrielle."

"They seem to love her too," Samuel adds, holding the door open for the others.

They make their way across the dark driveway to the barn, and a full moon moves out from behind a cloud to light their path. Jane tries to briefly relay what happened with the IIA.

Hershey and Samuel reach the goats at the same time. Gabrielle and the six baby goats are lumped together on a mound of hay. All are peacefully sleeping. Samuel puts his finger to his lips to signal quiet as the three sisters approach. Everyone smiles at the sight of innocence and pure love.

Magdalene is the only one to break the mood. "I wonder if she looks like her father."

Jane is about to scold her when a gigantic light forms in the middle of the barn. She prays that the roof is high enough. All eyes turn toward the light as it grows and grows into the large Luminescence.

"What is that?" Hershey whispers to Mimi.

"Eet eez zee angel father of Gabrielle," Mimi whispers back.

Samuel moves to Mimi. "That's an angel? I expected something different."

"So did I," Magdalene mutters.

The fully formed Luminescence finally fills the barn with his presence and resonance. "Stop the presses! I've found my daughter!"

Gabrielle wakes up and sees her father. She slowly lifts the mask off her head. A smaller version of her father's continuous hologram appears. She removes the gloves and blouse and a small feathered wingspan is finally free. After removing the rest of the clothes, she appears to be a mini version of her dad.

She walks out of the stall to her father. A flash of light explodes and swirls around and around the barn. The light tornado seems to dance up and down in a fluorescent rumba. First the light waves move to the ceiling and then down to the floor. They are like a slinky made of lightning. The undulating light dance is repeated over and over again.

Samuel and the others stand in awe, watching and waiting. The glowing dance concludes, and the familiar if not strange forms reappear. Gabrielle walks back to the huddled onlookers. She reaches out her feathery hand and touches Samuel's arm.

Samuel nods in understanding and turns to Hershey. "She wants to take the goats with her, but she's afraid you might miss them too much and be lonely?"

Hershey smiles at Gabrielle. "You gave those goats more love than anyone. They deserve to live with someone who appreciates them. If they want to go, it's okay with me."

Gabrielle's father joins her by the baby goats. They lower their heads as if talking to the goats. Suddenly a series of white lights emanate from each of the baby goats. The lights grow bigger and brighter, and the goats seem to fade into the light beams.

Gabrielle pulls on her father's leg feathers to get his attention.

"My daughter wishes to give the gift that keeps on giving to your leader."

Magdalene nudges Jane. "That would be you, Jane."

"Yes," Luminescence continues. "Yes, your guidance makes the heart grow fonder. Often, you have found the courage to go on even after much of life has held you back. You have searched for so long for someplace to call home sweet home. You have traveled like my daughter as an alien among many. For you can see the good and promise in others but not always in yourself. You have fallen many times and hurt yourself, but you always get back up. For all these things, Amoria gives you the gift of strong ankles, strong ankles, and strong ankles."

Jane smiles a knowing smile.

Amoria tugs on her father's feathers again, and he bends over for a new message. He stands tall and points to Mimi. "A smile shall always be your umbrella on a rainy, rainy day."

He points to Samuel. "Your kindness and love shall bring you peace. They always need a few good men, but it won't be you."

He moves to Magdalene. "Amoria likes the child inside you. She wants her to come out and play more. If you play more, your grandmother will be happy. Maybe you need more bran in your diet."

Both Luminescence and Amoria now turn to Hershey who stands directly under the overhead light. "We are not the messengers the world is waiting for," the father booms. "Someone is already here who brings harmony to this dissonant world. Someone listens with the ear of her heart, and if she can change one person in one small way, she can begin a transformation of everything. Love is not a secondhand emotion or a greeting card."

In unison, Amoria and Luminescence raise their feathers and point to Hershey. "You are love in a jar just waiting to be opened."

As one, they both turn and move to the middle of the barn. They raise their feathery arms, reaching skyward, and from the center of Amoria's small body comes a scratchy little voice sounding like an old worn record: "Thanks for the memory. We're so glad we had this time together. Good news and good night."

Amoria looks to her father and the multicolored lightning bolt returns with a quick bright flash, and they both are gone. The barn is dark except for the bare bulb over Hershey's head. After a short silence, the three nuns, Hershey, and Samuel walk out into the moonlight.

No one wants to discuss what just happened, so Samuel tries a new subject. "Do you think you'll ever see Sean and Shakeeta again?" He asks Magdalene.

"Oh yes. I'll see them next week," Magdalene answers. "They called us from their home in Cleveland before we came to the farm. They have to testify at the secret IIA hearings in Washington, and Jane and I also need to testify. We plan to meet them there."

"So all the mysteries are solved." Hershey's says, sounding rather bittersweet as she leads them toward the cars.

"Not all of them." Jane turns to Samuel. "I think you and I should spend some time sharing your concerns. Important life decisions shouldn't be borne alone. I just never felt you were ready to talk about your needs until now, or I would have encouraged a discussion. I think your journey back to your feelings has brought you to a fork in the road." She gives him a quick hug, and then turns to Hershey. "Sister Hershey, will you be coming back to Syracuse with us?"

Hershey doesn't look at Jane. She just shakes her head. "No. I need some time to decide if I'm Sky Volta or Mary Margaret, or if I should legally change my name to Hershey Ghirardelli. I feel like I'm little parts of each personality, but I've never been put together. I don't want Sky's life. I'm through with drugs and drinking. Mary Margaret didn't feel real to me either. She lived with more drama than Sky did. Mary Margaret never fit in with her proper, conforming and fiercely dysfunctional family. Maybe I need to be nobody for awhile. The amnesia was a kind of blessing. It erased everything, so I have a chance for a fresh start."

She takes a few more steps and continues. "I really understood Gabrielle. I knew what she was feeling. She wanted what would be good for her, her true self. She wanted to return to where she's not an alien. I'm tired of feeling that alienation too. I think I need time to find out who I really am. The farm feels like a good place to do that. Sorry to leave an empty place at the table."

"Oh, chère." Mimi catches up to Hershey. "The place eez not empty for long. Sister Culberth arrives tomorrow from San Francisco, and we wheel go back to France together."

Hershey is amazed at how things are working out. She stops to share a hug with Mimi. Mimi takes the small cross from around her neck and puts it over Hershey's head. "This wheel protect you, chère, when I am not around." Mimi turns and catches up to Magdalene.

Jane moves closer to Hershey, and they link arms. "You know," Jane says thoughtfully. "I've decided to leave my leadership role in the Community after our Annual Assembly in Iowa. I think it's time I do a little integrating myself. I've been so busy trying to lead others to their truth that I may have forgotten about myself. I think a nice long retreat is in order, perhaps someplace with a pastoral setting. I'll bet the daylight sky around these hills is beautiful. Nature is so good for integrating and healing, even for making future plans."

She catches Hershey's look and winks. "You know Hershey, it's not unusual today for more and more women to enter religious communities later in life even after they've had successful careers." They both laugh and keep walking.

Joan Albarella, a University of Buffalo Professor Emeritus, is author of the Niki Barnes Mystery Series: *Close To You, Called to Kill,* and *Agenda for Murder.* She is also the author of four books of poetry (*Mirror Me; Poems For the Asking; Women, Flowers, Fantasy;* and *Spirit and Joy*), two plays (*Mother Cabrini's Mission to America* and *Katharine Hepburn's Brownies*), and over 200 articles, biographies, poems, and short stories. She is a member of Mystery Writers of America, Sisters in Crime, Poets and Writers, and the Italian American Writers Association. She lives in Western New York.